A SWIRL of OCEAN

ALSO BY MELISSA SARNO

Just Under the Clouds

A SWIRL of OCEAN

MELISSA SARNO

Alfred A. Knopf
New York

THIS IS A BORZOI BOOK PUBLISHED BY ALFRED A. KNOPF

Knopf, Borzoi Books, and the colophon are registered trademarks of Penguin Random House LLC.

Visit us on the Web! rhcbooks.com

Educators and librarians, for a variety of teaching tools, visit us at
RHTeachersLibrarians.com

Library of Congress Cataloging-in-Publication Data is available upon request.
ISBN 978-1-5247-2012-4 (trade) — ISBN 978-1-5247-2013-1 (lib. bdg.) —
ISBN 978-1-5247-2014-8 (ebook)

The text of this book is set in 12.25-point Horley Old Style MT.

Printed in the United States of America
August 2019
10 9 8 7 6 5 4 3 2 1
First Edition

For Mom and Dad

HIGH TIDE, 11:06 A.M.

"It's way too cold." Lindy slings her boots over her shoulder and skirts the ocean water as fast she can, her toes and their chipped polish dancing away.

I stand flat-footed at the shore, letting the cool water wash over my feet. "Scaredy-cat."

Lindy laughs, but then she gets the look she always gets in her eyes when we're together at the water. Something sad and far-off. Something I can't get at. She always says you can't trust the ocean.

When I wondered why someone who didn't trust the ocean lived right up next to it, she only said it's better to keep a close eye on something you can't trust.

Maybe it has something to do with Lindy finding me here ten years ago. Right on this shore.

She saw me in the morning, my hair wet and wound with seaweed as I sat on the beach. I was two years old. She

1

was twenty. I wore nothing but my moon snail necklace and a bathing suit. There was no one up or down the sand. She called the paramedics first, to make sure I was okay. Then the police. They took me to the hospital, where the doctors examined me and the detectives asked their questions. They sat me on an examination table, and I banged my feet against the tinny base. Lindy said the clanging set her own heart racing; she was scared they wouldn't figure out where I came from and then scared because she knew I was already where I belonged. With her. And what did she know about taking care of a two-year-old?

But the days, she said, kept warming me toward her, the way I took her pinkie and led her around, the way I emptied her jigsaw puzzles and spread myself in the pieces, shrieking as I tossed them up like snow. She said I guided her to the shore and crouched down low, scooping up sand and shells, and pointing at seagulls. That was the thing, she said, about being only a couple years in and brand-new to the world. I came and let her see it new.

Still, I've asked her a thousand times why she took me, a girl alive but left for dead. She always smiles, says it like it's nothing, "I figured you were mine."

And I have been hers, ever since, my whole life, but for two years when I was somebody nobody else seems to have known.

As I sink deeper and deeper into the sand, Lindy's elbows jut from her stick arms and her bony hips tick from side to side. She never let me call her *Mom* because she always said the two of us were more like sisters than anything else. But we're eighteen years apart and I look nothing like her. *Solid rock* is what she calls me. Others call me *sturdy*. Lindy, on the other hand, is like some kind of twig ready to snap. Her hair is as short as mine is long, all spiky and stick-uppy and not caring which direction it's going. She wears a leather cuff at her wrist and all black no matter how sunny it is. My boy shorts and breezy hair seem so plain next to her.

She drops her lace-up boots in the bucket. I hear the shells clack against the tin.

I snatch the bucket from her hands and sigh. "I think I'm done for the season." It's the middle of September, and I only sold one shell necklace for the day. An oyster shell I painted turquoise with gold trim.

The breeze yawns over me just as the sun looks away. Everybody else might be gone until next summer, but we live here year-round, on the long, skinny strip of land we call *ours,* between the ocean and the bay. The ocean is the only thing coming and the only thing going.

"So, what are you thinking?" she asks.

I know what she's asking without her having to say, the same thing she's been wondering since she first brought it up yesterday, about Elder Glynn and his yapping dog moving in with us.

I don't know. I mean, she used to say there was never

anyone in Barnes Bluff that she would give the time of day, and now all of a sudden she's talking about a boyfriend moving in.

I want to tell her *it's fine.* I want to make her happy. But *Elder*? I don't understand why she's leaving it up to me.

"Don't you think there's something a little funny about him?" I ask.

"He makes me laugh," she offers.

"I mean funny-strange. That kind of funny."

"Everybody's strange."

"He can't even control his eight-pound dog," I say.

She laughs.

I swallow hard. "Wouldn't it be better if he left us alone?"

She frowns. "I don't know. We've been alone for a long time, Summer."

"I like it that way," I say.

"Well, we don't have to decide right now," she says.

I can tell she's disappointed, but she forces a little smile. "Come on." She reaches for my hand, and we walk to the boardwalk.

Usually we'd visit the souvenir shops and browse T-shirts, then point out the weirdest ones we could find. I still have a worn-out tee of a hamburger and hot dog holding hands, and I half snorted when Lindy named the burger *Patty.* But the shops are already closed for the season, and the boardwalk is nearly empty. A tall man stands

4

at a wooden post, overlooking the beach. He's out of place in a corduroy blazer, with a notebook sticking out of the breast pocket.

Lindy watches him, her brow furrowed.

"What?" I wonder out loud.

Words stick to her tongue, then she shakes her head like she's shaking off sand. She shrugs and turns away from the stranger. Her eyes brighten like a little kid's, because Lindy may look like she's all bone-sharp and full of jagged angles, but she's mush-soft inside.

I know what she's thinking before she says it.

"We could get glitter moon sprinkles." She grins.

"Purple pumpkin," I offer.

"Buttercream sea foam."

"Sunbeam buttercrunch."

"Popsicle rainbow."

"Ham and egg Cracker Jack?"

Lindy wrinkles her nose with a "No thank you," and we both bust out laughing as we climb the steps to the board-walk toward Old Crocker's ice cream cart, where none of our made-up flavors are ever there and Crocker scoops vanilla or chocolate only. There are no swirls or sprinkles or even cones. And the ice cream comes in a flimsy tan cup with a wooden spoon.

But Crocker grabs our quarters with his soft, shaky hands and knows without us having to say that I want vanilla and Lindy wants chocolate, and, somehow, when it melts on our tongues, it is the creamiest, sweetest-tasting ice cream we've ever had.

Lindy happy-groans as she takes her first bite, and we both sink to the bench, right next to his weathered umbrella, because you can't eat Old Crocker's ice cream unless you're sitting down.

I set the bucket at our bare feet and let the cool vanilla slide down my throat.

"You closing up shop?" Lindy asks.

Crocker's voice is quiet. "Tomorrow."

"We'll miss you," I say.

There's not a hint of a smile past his cracked lips, just his way of looking up and out at the sand, the shore, and the sky. "I'll be back."

I tuck my head on Lindy's shoulder and breathe the smooth salty air.

Once I'm done with my ice cream, I wander by myself to Gramzy's Pitch & Putt, banging the bell a bunch of times, my signal to Jeremiah that it's me.

Wire buckets of golf balls hang from the ceiling like houseplants, all the colors of the rainbow. I always pick purple. Lindy calls it *the color of royalty. Fit for a queen.*

I jump to my tiptoes and peek into the game room, which is connected by a little glass window to the hut. Jeremiah traipses past the air-hockey board, his hair sticking up wild. You'd think he just woke up, but that's the way it always is, a bird's nest around his ears.

Then he swings open the adjoining door, marching barefoot right on past me. Fishhooks dangle from the belt loop of his jeans, like always, and he carries a crooked fishing rod. "Good. You're here. Got something to show you."

I don't ask any questions. Jeremiah's always got something to show somebody, and as he marches on, the door nearly knocks me in the chin as he steps out into the sunlight.

He leads me up onto the little golf course, which nobody's using now that summer's done. We climb the bunker around hole number four, pushing past the beach grass and out into the dunes.

Our feet sink in and out of the squishy sand, and it feels a little like riding a pogo stick as we slip in and pop back up.

Jeremiah stops and uses his fishing rod to point to a little mound in the sand.

I kneel in closer. It's the blackish hump of a turtle. This is the fourth one we've found in two days. The shell is a pattern of diamonds, and it's marked with a big yellow dot, just like all the others. But all the others were dead, according to Jeremiah's Gramzy, who pretty much knows everybody's current status in Barnes Bluff.

This one's stretching its crinkly neck.

I look at the tag dangling at its feet. "Four, seven, dash, three," I read out loud.

I know what Jeremiah's thinking before he can say anything, both of us looking over the beach grass at his neighbor's place.

"Turtle Lady," I say, looking at her house next door.

If you're a kid in Barnes Bluff, you know Turtle Lady

but you don't see her. She's a scientist, and she's got an overgrown mess of a backyard and a house with all the windows shut up. Even the adults in Barnes Bluff think she's creepy. Lindy always hugs her chest whenever anyone mentions Turtle Lady's name or we pass her house.

Gramzy said she used to travel all over the world studying amphibians. I guess being a traveling scientist suits someone who doesn't like people much. But ever since I've known her she's shut herself inside and doesn't come out. All we know about Turtle Lady are her turtles. They've got blobs of paint and numbered tags at their feet. And everybody calls her *Turtle Lady* because she's just that kind of legend.

"She can't go around leaving turtles all over. We should stake out her place until she leaves the house," I say. "You got anywhere to be?"

Jeremiah shakes his head.

"Me neither."

He lightly taps his fishing rod on the turtle shell. "What about this little thing?"

"Four seven three?"

"Mm-hmm."

"You got a cardboard box?"

We carry 47–3 in a shoebox with poked holes and a half-eaten strawberry, setting up at hole number nine so we've got the best view. From here we're face to face with Turtle Lady's side yard. We can see her front steps and the driveway if a car pulled away. Jeremiah's got a jumbo jar of pickles in case we get hungry. I lean back on my elbows, letting the overgrown grass tickle my shoulders.

I hear the ocean just past the dunes and get to thinking about Lindy's question again. "I still haven't answered her," I tell Jeremiah, who nods, carefully, ready to listen to whatever rambling I need to do. "I mean . . . *Elder?* I like our family the way it is."

"That dog is pretty terrible," he reminds me.

"I *know.*"

He scrunches up his nose. "And the whole fish hatchery thing?"

"His job's a total hazard." I groan.

"Face it. He reeks."

"Right?" I agree. "It's lethal."

"But Lindy likes him," he reminds me.

"Lindy likes him." I sigh.

"It will make her happy."

I know he's right. "It will."

I peek in on 47–3. Its little head pokes out like a scared tulip pushing through old winter dirt. Then I look toward Turtle Lady's sun-washed beach house. All the shingles are battered gray from the salty air.

"What do you think she's doing in there?" I ask.

"Four seven three?"

I shake my head. "Turtle Lady."

"Experiments," he says, like he's sure of it.

I think of the experiments we do in Mrs. Grady's science class. She says she's got two "shows" that bring the "audience." Shows meaning lessons. Audience meaning us.

Baking soda volcanoes.

And Coca-Cola and Mentos.

Everything else is the boring stuff like planting a seed and waiting for it to grow. I'm doing a moldy bread experiment because Lindy did it when she was my age and thought it would be a good idea. I figured it would be all gauzy and puffed and blue-green-gross, but it's brought me nothing but stale bread.

"Well, this stakeout is about as exciting as watching paint dry." I set the shoebox down and stand up, kicking at the bunker. Sand spits up from my dusty flip-flops. "If I can get to the top of the fence, do you think I could reach the window?"

"And do what?" Jeremiah asks. "Climb in?"

"Maybe there's something we're missing at this angle. Maybe there's a way of seeing in. Spot me," I say before he can argue.

I run to the wooden fence and climb up.

Jeremiah stands below me. With his skinny legs and his bony wrists, elbows jutting out like knives, he's got to be just about the worst spotter I can think of. Scrawny's good for relay races or squeezing in the back seat of a car. Not for spotting kids falling from fences.

I'm still too far from the window. The screen has this way of dusting over whatever's inside. But as I look in, I catch a glint of silver-something, and then I see the sun catch it, and there are sausage-link fingers on the sill, stretching up to a big doughy face and two squinty eyes staring right at me.

I launch from the fence like I'm in some Sunday funny, blasting to the grass, where I fall to my hands. My palms sting. "She's in there," I say, catching my breath. "At the window." My hair hangs to the grass as I crouch, and Jeremiah looks from me to the window to the pickle jar clutched at his chest.

Then he screws the lid off and shoves his fist in the jar. "Come and get your turtles!" he yells.

He starts flinging pickles at the window. One after the other, like he's on automatic. They hit the glass and slide from it, leaving pickle juice stains.

"What the heck are you doing?" I shout.

Jeremiah shakes his head, like some crazed thing. "Come and get 'em!"

Before I know what I'm doing, I plunge my hand into the jar, fishing for pickles. I jump up on a plastic beach chair to get my aim right, then I toss a fistful of pickles at the window. They slap against the glass like oversized coins. As they slip down, there's something that makes me feel good about what I'm doing, something that makes me feel like I'm saying, *Come out, quit hiding, come and get your turtles and go.*

Until I watch the shadow behind the screen shift.

Turtle Lady is on the move.

I stop just as Jeremiah slams another pickle at the sticky, wet windowpane.

The curtain falls.

"Stop," I say out loud. "She's coming."

Jeremiah sets his jar on the ground. Pickle juice sloshes over onto the dirt. He steps up on my chair, and we're both eye level with the tip of the fence, waiting.

We hear the side door slam before we see her. Black clogs bang at the pebbled steps. She's got thick, busting calves. A housedress that matches her curtains. And snow-white hair stuck at the top of her head like a gauzy ball of yarn. There's that dough face again and two stink-eyes stuffed in her face like raisins.

I think she's about to say something. Then I see the long garden hose dangling from her hand like a snake. Before I can react, water's gushing at my face and I can't see a thing.

Jeremiah squeals and jumps from the chair, knocking me straight off. Water sprays at my back as I try to stand up from the grass, then it gets in my eyes again.

Jeremiah and I run like mad, my hair sopping, flip-flops slipping from my feet, running to the Pitch & Putt hut and out of this lady's way.

Our shoes slap against the floor of the wooden hut, and we duck under the hanging baskets, into the game room, where I throw myself on the old velvet couch.

"What in the heck?" Jeremiah grumbles, chest heaving as he leans against a foosball table.

"What are you throwing pickles for?" I scold.

"You did it, too!"

"She's totally nutters," I say.

I squish deeper into the couch. It looks like someone threw up flowers on it, that's how ugly and splotchy and weird it is. Everything in the room feels basement-old, made up of things you want to forget you have.

Jeremiah's Gramzy charges a dollar a day to get into

the game room. In the summer, when it rains, parents dump their kids out here like a box of crayons, everybody spilling out all over the floor, fighting over old games like Hungry Hungry Hippos and the missing pieces of Candy Land. Off-season, it looks like everything in Barnes Bluff Bay: used, empty, and left behind.

I slow my breath, flip my wet hair, and kick my dirty bare feet on the arm of the couch. "She's up to something," I warn. "But what?"

He shrugs. "Dunno. We're gonna find out, though, right?"

"Course."

"She's reeeeal defensive." Jeremiah sloshes around in his Converse sneakers, fishhooks jangling from his jeans. "I mean, we're just kids. She could've drowned us."

I roll my eyes. "Well, I don't know about that." I pull the leg of my shorts up. "But she made me skin my knee."

"She's a menace to society."

"Nutters," I repeat.

"A hose-spraying, reptile-killing, knee-skinning, house-crazy *Turtle Lady*."

I sit up fast. "Four seven three," I remember out loud. "Did you grab the box?"

Jeremiah shakes his head. "No, did you?"

"Shoot."

Then we put our fingers to our noses.

"Not it!" we call out at the same time.

We both look to the door of the hut, like Turtle Lady's going to come barging in with her fat calves and her clogs.

"We can't just leave the poor thing there," I say.

"But what if we get hosed again?"

I think of that tossed-aside turtle. The only one we've found alive. I sigh. "I'll do it. Lindy's expecting me home, anyway."

"Puzzle time?" Jeremiah asks.

I nod. Lindy and I have a thousand-piece puzzle we're making our way through. It's an ocean jumble. Waves, coral, and all the fish you can imagine. They're glossy and rainbow-colored, soaked in a big bright sun from up above. It looks like the word *ocean*. What you might picture in your head. Not like it really is, cloudy, dark, and unknowable.

I stand up to leave, flipping my wet hair over my shoulder.

Jeremiah says, "See ya." He doesn't even have to say *tomorrow*. That's just the way it goes.

I swing open the door to the hut. The spring's so loose, it hangs in midair. Might never close. So I kick it, like always, and walk around the flag-waving Pitch & Putt to hole number nine.

I keep my eye on Turtle Lady's side door, those wrinkled, old steps, where she stood with her hand poised on the silver handle, ready to hose us. But she's gone. And when I make my way to the shoebox, I see that 47–3 is, too. The box is on its side, and 47–3 is nowhere in sight, which is saying a lot for a turtle who can't get too far too fast.

I wander the course for a little bit, watching where I step. I stop at the beach chair. The butt of the seat is all droopy from Jeremiah and me standing on it. But I stand on it again, because I can't do the chair more harm than I've already done, and I watch the stained window, which has been rained on by sticky, wet pickles. I feel a little bad until my ripped-up knee stings again.

Beyond the window it's dark and screened in, and the curtain is still. But I see the silver shine of her ring on the windowsill, her big old sausage fingers, and I jump from the chair and take off running.

don't stop until I get to our place, which is stilted, peel-
ing, and faded. The beach grass sways as I climb up the
tall stairs to the rickety porch. It ribbons around the house
with stairs to the beach.

The bungalow looks like one big old wooden square,
with a tiny triangle sitting on top like a sailor's cap. Inside,
the wallpaper's flowered and the tablecloth's covered in
cherries, with curtains stained by the sun. It's mismatched
and cluttered, all my stuff tripping over itself. Lindy's
always hounding me to get rid of things, because I hold
on to everything. She thinks a roof over our heads and a
steady diet of cigarettes and coffee are enough to survive.
But everything here has its place. If I lift a thing, it leaves
a ring of dust to remember it by.

I set the empty shoebox on the table and peek at my

stale bread. Nothing. Not one single fuzz. But it sits there like it's pleased with itself.

Lindy calls out, "Summer, that you?"

All I can think is, *Who else would it be?*

"We're out on the back porch!" she calls.

We. Elder must be here.

I slap the screen door open. My flip-flops thump the rattling wood planks as I loop around.

I hear the yapping first.

Elder's dog, Elsa, is squawking like a sick bird, growling and barking her head off as she hops from her leash, which, as she sets off, snaps her back in place and only makes the little gremlin yip louder.

I smell the quick whiff of fish, which means Elder must have showered after work. If he hadn't, it would be much worse. He shoots up from a wicker patio chair, trying to shush Elsa. She's baring her teeth. This tiny furball with cartoon Dumbo ears thinks she can take us. She must have what my history teacher, Miss Dillweather, calls *a Napoleon complex.* A shorty-pants who's got to prove she's a giant.

Elder is the opposite. Giraffe-tall. He bends over like a sheet folding itself in half, and I'm afraid he'll snap at the waist.

"Summer, hey." He laughs nervously, yanking at the jumpy dog, who is still growling, all low and rumbly.

I nod a *hey*, thinking, if I ignore him, he'll disappear. I have no idea what Lindy sees in him. She's bunched up in a mismatched chair, an ocean-wave tattoo swirling up her arm, while he's straightening his smudged glasses and a crooked necktie.

Lindy's legs are curled under her. She's got a cigarette, and smoke rises up as the evening sky tries to push its way into view.

When she sees me, she smashes the cigarette butt into an old ashtray and wafts the smoke away. She's been trying to quit forever. She always says this pack's her last. So I sneak cigarettes away and hide them at the soggy wet bottom of the outdoor trash until the pack empties. But, instead of quitting, she buys another from the Citgo at the wharf, and we play the game all over again.

Her chin rests at her knee. "How's Jeremiah?"

"Same as always. Wandering around poking at things."

"What'd you do?"

"Turtle Lady hosed us," I say, straight, because news in Barnes Bluff leaks fast.

"*Miss Ellis* hosed you?" Lindy asks.

Lindy's always been weird about Turtle Lady. She's the only one I know who even calls her *Miss Ellis*. "Yes. *Actually* hosed us. Like, took a hose to my face." I display my wet clothes and shake my damp hair.

Lindy looks concerned. She knows me too well. "What'd you do?"

"Threw pickles at her window."

Her eyes get large.

"Jeremiah started it. Plus. She deserves it. She's killing turtles."

Elder stands up straight. "Turtle Lady is a fine—"

"She's killing turtles," I repeat to Lindy. "She's got to take responsibility."

"I hate to tell you, but I don't think throwing pickles at her is the answer."

"At her *window*," I correct. "Not *her*."

She narrows her eyes. "Same difference."

"Well, one's a person and one's a pane of gl—"

Lindy interrupts, her voice rising. "Same. Difference. Don't mess with Miss Ellis," she scolds. She gazes over in the direction of her house. "Just leave her alone."

I slump into a striped chair and kick my feet up on the table. Lindy's got saltines and a hunk of bright yellow cheese out, so I dig right in. We both think cheese and crackers is a totally acceptable dinner. There's also a jug of something called CARLO ROSSI and waxy little paper cups, like you gargle mouthwash with, but, instead of Listerine, they're filled with whatever red stuff's in the jug. Pretty sure it's wine, which Lindy doesn't drink. But I watch her take a sip and purse her lips like she's tasted something sour.

Elder stands, holding on tight to the leash, watching Lindy, and his face breaks out into a giant grin. Then he swirls the red stuff in his paper cup, takes a big sniff with his nose, and gives a thumbs-up while he sips.

He's always finding ways to impress me less.

"Have you heard of a *Spirula* shell?" he asks. Elder knows I've got my shell collecting, so he loves to start in, trying to be all friendly. He thinks we've got something in common, just because he works with fish. *Shells* are not *fish*.

"No," I force myself to say.

"It's not like your gastropods, ya know, your snails and your slugs and all that. It's from a ram's horn squid. The coils don't touch." He circles his finger on the table in a spiral motion.

It bugs me that I'm a little bit curious. "Where can you find it?"

"Not here. In tropical waters. It's the only species of its kind. Most people haven't seen them. They've only seen what washes up. The shell." He spirals his finger on the table and grins, again, like he's about to laugh. But he doesn't.

It sounds pretty amazing, but I don't want to make too big a deal of it, so I just nod and say, "Cool."

"Nerd," Lindy teases.

He smirks.

I watch them, their pink cheeks, their matching smiles, the way they're looking at each other like the space between them is all that matters.

I stand up fast and make a clanking at the table when I do. It feels a little like I'm trying to break a spell that's already done its magic. "I'm going swimming," I say, waiting for Lindy to stop and scold me and remind me that night swimming's against the rules.

Instead, she nods. "Uh-huh, okay." Then she untangles her legs, rocks forward, and offers Elder a hunk of plasticky cheese.

It's a clear evening as I walk to the shore. There's still some time before the sun sets, but it's cold, which means the ocean will feel warmer, even if the fall season is picking up speed. I wear my too-small bikini, with the bottoms bunching up and the back strap digging into my flesh. I march in fast, my knees above the surface. Then I wade in, and the coolness shocks my bare stomach. My whole body shivers in goose pimples, but I know the faster you get in, the faster you get used to being cold, until your body warms right up.

I swim out to where the sandbar drops away. I can tell by the way the water darkens, and I let my feet slip over the line. Some people hate knowing they can't touch the bottom, but I love the feeling of emptiness beneath my toes. It feels like a world of beginnings with no end.

It was Lindy who taught me to swim. We practiced for

weeks in the calm of the bay. She held her arms underneath my belly and I floated there, kicking and kicking, keeping my chin above the surf. One day, she let go, without me even knowing. Instead of sinking, I soared ahead, skimming the water like a shark. Even now, I feel the memory of the way she held me. It makes me feel strong.

I float on my back and watch an entire blue sky melt toward yellow and orange and dark.

Before I know it, I'm tossed.

Rip current.

A tide torn in half. One piece of ocean curling toward the other in a straight line instead of toward the shore.

There aren't even warnings for this kind of ocean trick. You could know the sea better than anything, like I do, and still get stuck toeing the line, just trying to keep your chin up toward the sky.

I hear Lindy's voice in my head: *Stay calm. Don't fight it. You won't win.*

But I'm chest-deep and I can't even feel the bottom. I can't walk my way out. The shore's right there and, at the same time, it's a zillion miles away. I keep my eye on it.

I try to move forward. I bring one arm up and over the water, let it tickle the surface, then push the rest of the ocean away. I breathe. I lift the other arm and do the same. I try to force myself forward, but I'm completely and totally stuck.

Most people think you should swim parallel to the

shore when you're caught in a riptide, but Lindy says you have to stay put. You have to tread water and wait it out until the ocean decides to carry you in.

I close my eyes and stay in one place, moving my arms and legs until my muscles ache. I remember Lindy's arms at my waist.

I put my faith in surrender.

Take me, I want to say. *Go right ahead.*

Then I swallow a ton of ocean. I'm so full, I could burst. Lungs exploding. Eyes stinging.

I cough up what I can and let the rest take me.

don't know how it happens. But I end up at the shore, seaweed choking my wrists. Lindy's hunched at my side in seconds. She's got this way of always having her eye out for me in the ocean, even when I think she's busying herself somewhere else.

She wraps her arms around my waist, and I feel safe. "What happened?" she asks.

"It's okay," I sputter. "It's fine. I wasn't drowning or anything. I knew what I was doing. I—"

"You know the rip currents are bad this time of year," she interrupts.

"I—"

"Have you lost your mind?"

"I told you where I was going. You seemed to think it was okay just a few minutes ago."

She shushes me. Then she grabs my hand and pulls me up. "Let's get you inside."

I breathe in, my lungs wet with sea, as Lindy leads me toward the house.

"You'll catch your death of cold." She shakes her head, tossing a towel on my shoulders.

"Death isn't *catchable*," I argue as the towel slips.

"Oh, it isn't, is it?"

"Nope."

"Well, you tell that to death sometime. The rest of us'll be laughing six feet under." She lifts the towel back to my shoulders.

I stand up straighter, my cheeks hot with windburn, my body deciding between warm and cold.

"You know I don't like you swimming this late in the day," she says. "You could drown, kiddo."

"I know how to swim!" I strike back. I can swim forever. *Born swimming,* Lindy says. I slip the towel up to my chin.

"Just . . . be careful, Summer. You're all I've got."

"Well, I've got homework," I say. "Loads of it. You can have some if you want."

She laughs, and I try to smile. But it isn't even true, me being all she has. I mean, now she's got Elder, too.

The way they look at each other. They're in *like*. Or whatever. Fine. In *love*. That's what she's been saying, anyway.

I look around the deck. The cheese is crusty from sitting out. The saltines pack is empty. "Where's Elder?"

"Home."

I think of Lindy and me living in this house on stilts all these years. We have always felt like a special secret, the two of us, chanting imaginary ice cream flavors and laughing at corny T-shirts. Lindy might only tolerate the beach during the day, but we've always loved it together at night. We used to walk to the edge of the point and sit side by side, our legs dangling from the tall rocks as the water rushed below. It seems silly now, but we'd close our eyes at the same time and send our wishes to the stars. I'd let my heart ask for longer summers. When I wondered what Lindy wished for, she didn't keep it secret, the way I did; she'd say something that would always surprise me, like how she wanted a sailboat.

For a long time, I didn't need any kids my own age. It was Jeremiah who marched up to our back porch one summer when I was eight, fishhooks jangling from his jeans like wind chimes, asking me if I wanted to *see something*. The first day he showed me a lost crab's leg. The next he took me to a swarm of minnows at the shallow end of the ocean. And it became part of every day from then on, one of us wandering over to the other, with something to show or see or do.

But he was the only one we let into our family of two.

Until now.

Until Elder Glynn swept on through the restaurant Lindy waitresses at, sitting at the oyster counter, slurping down one oyster after the next, tired of living in an apartment in the city, a *shoebox*, he called it, so he came here to slow down for a while and work at the fish hatchery. Slowing down, screeching to a halt, onto our back porch, into the space between Lindy's big brown eyes and the sky she's gazing up at.

I sigh and we both reach for our moon snail necklaces, because sometimes we do things like that, decide things in sync. I made hers from old rope and smooth purple moon snail shells. I made it to match mine. It's the only thing I have from when she found me. The one link to my past. And I've extended it, over the years, with rope and twine, so it fits an older me. We fiddle with them all the time, but we never take them off.

I sigh. "Okay."

"Okay?"

She knows what I'm saying without me having to explain. "He's kind, Summer. And smart."

I scrunch up my nose. "I guess."

"You'll still have your own room, and we'll all be on our own schedules. Elder will still be working at the hatchery. And I'll be at the restaurant. You'll have school. And we'll come and go like we always do, sharing the chores and dinner, like it's always been."

"Right." I force a smile.

She frowns. "You don't believe me."

"I guess I knew it couldn't be *forever*. Just you and me."

She places her hands on both of my shoulders. "It's always forever."

I nod and try to agree, but it gnaws at me, this feeling I sometimes get at the pit of me. That I'm not *really* hers. That she's not *really* mine.

Even if the adoption was final before I could make my own memories. Even if she laid out the papers as soon as I was old enough to understand so I could see it all. A set of *unknown* parents whose *rights* were *terminated*. Not a runaway or an orphan. A *foundling* in a case that reached dead end after dead end. And, even when I went through that phase, when I was a kid, like I was some Harriet the Spy, researching libraries and microfilms, interviewing everyone I could, in a town small enough for someone to maybe, *maybe*, know my own story before I did. Even when I found nothing. Even in a case as good as closed, I know there's still a file in a cabinet somewhere.

Someone left me behind.

Couldn't Lindy?

I dismiss the thought as soon as I have it. She would never.

Lindy stands up, and I follow. I can tell we're both done with the day, and I leave a trail of ocean as we slip through the screen door and climb the narrow stairs together.

In my room, there are piles of clothes, and books sit on

31

their sides on the crooked shelves. Rows of my seashell collection line the knobby wooden desk where I do my jewelry-making. I've got a bunch of wicker baskets filled with their weathered, fanned-out shapes.

She spins her arm around. "You should think of sorting through these."

"What for?" I ask.

"One of these days I'm going to turn on the television and see you on one of those hoarding shows," she teases.

I go through a messy drawer, looking for an old tee to sleep in.

Lindy's eyes brighten. "Ooh, wear my favorite," she urges.

I rummage for the wrinkled blue cotton and hold it over my too-tight bathing suit. It has a faded coconut in a rocket ship and the word *Coconaut*.

She giggles. "Gets me every time."

I stand a little shivery and roll my eyes. Then I slip it on over my suit. It's not like I can strip right here in front of Lindy like I used to do when I was a little kid.

I collapse to the bed, wrapping my arms up against my chest. She grabs a brush from my messy dresser and runs it through my tangled hair. Even if I'm old enough to brush my hair myself, it feels nice, like I could shed a worry away with each stroke.

"Your bread's on the kitchen counter," Lindy reminds me. "It's not doing a thing."

"Nope. Too many preservatives," I groan.

"We're the only people I know wishing food would spoil faster."

"How long did it take for yours to grow mold?" I ask.

She shakes her head. "I can't remember. I remember the science fair in the auditorium. I remember getting a blue ribbon. I remember taking it home to my mother, who put it in a little tin box, a forever keepsake." Her voice fades. I wish she'd say more. Lindy so rarely talks about her life before me. She always flicks away her past like it's this unwanted thing.

"Well, I don't think one fuzzy green patch is too much to ask," I say.

"It'll get there, kiddo. It's got to. The little loaf that could." She smiles, twirls the dry ends of my hair, and pats them in place on my back. Then she kisses my head and stands up. "No more night swimming," she reminds me.

I nod as she turns to leave, and I hear her patter on the steps.

I stare at the ceiling, at the swirl of glow-in-the-dark stars Lindy and me stuck up there a few years ago. They're losing their shine as the memory of light fades away.

I turn to my desk. A half-made string of beaded shells sits unfinished. I should clasp it, end it, store it until I start selling again next summer. Instead, I feel heavy and sick as I watch the breeze nag at the curtains. The ocean I swallowed sits at the pit of my belly.

I close my eyes. The pit of me gets wider and wider, and it fills up more and more. Ocean washes through me, and I scatter outside of it like a worried crab. Until I'm dreaming a dream so big, it takes over into the night. I dream a girl.

HIGH TIDE, 11:05 P.M.

Tink sat in a plastic chair. The ocean waves crashed and fell away, again and again, and her feet slid deeper and deeper into the sand. She closed her eyes.

It was the Fourth of July, Independence Day, and sparklers flickered across the beach. The kids streamed and swirled them against the darkening sky. But Tink didn't want a dumb sparkler, didn't want to listen to Kimmy Forrester all giggly and shrieking while Len chased after her with fire, didn't want Alexis rolling her eyes at everything she said, acting like they weren't even sisters, like Tink was some stray pet no one wanted to claim.

All Tink wanted was to be alone.

But Kimmy was already at her side, all breathy and laugh-y, her hand at Tink's wrist as she slapped her bare feet in the wet sand. "They're gonna start the fireworks," Kimmy said. "Come on."

Tink let her wrist fall limp in Kimmy's hands. She shook her head.

"We're gonna set 'em off ourselves," Kimmy insisted.

Tink sighed and opened her eyes to Kimmy's wild hair, its frizz all soaked in moonlight. "Ourselves?" she asked.

"Rockets," said Kimmy. "You in?"

"Who's going to?" Tink asked.

"Whoever wants to. The moms are fixing dessert back at the house. They won't even notice. Come on." Kimmy took off, darting across the beach to the bonfire, where everybody was set up on beach blankets holding soda cans wrapped in soft cozies. Alexis was there. Her hair fell like silk to her knees.

Tink pulled the sleeves of her hoodie over her fingertips and stood up. There was no use in pretending nobody else existed. They had the rest of the summer to get through, on this one stretch of beach, which used to feel like magic to her but was now weirdly charged with Kimmy all gross and gooey over Len, and Alexis spending all her days with her not-quite-a boyfriend, but not-quite-*not*-a boyfriend, Coop, and working across the bay at the arcade.

Tink couldn't decide where to sit. Alexis was usually out somewhere. And when she was around, she was off to the side, twirling her hair, pretending she wasn't part of an "us" anymore. But there she was, in the middle of things again, her eyes smiling.

Tink took her chance.

She sat right next to Alexis so their knees were touching.

Tink expected Alexis to scoot over quick, groan on about why she was always *hanging all over* her. Instead, Alexis slid her arm through hers, wrapped herself up with Tink, like they did every year watching their dad shoot off fireworks, and it felt, to Tink, like they were who they'd always been. Sisters, yes. But more than that, too. A secret, the two of them together, that no one else could get at.

Len and his father were hanging by Tink and Alexis's dad, so Kimmy was there, too—where else would she be? The four of them sorted through boxes of fireworks. The three moms were inside, like Kimmy said, and Tink could see them up at the house, at the window screen, laughing like the schoolgirl friends they liked to remind all the kids they used to be before they grew up, got families, and rented a house every summer in Barnes Bluff Bay.

Tink settled in, Alexis's arm still linked with hers. Maybe she wouldn't have to disappear. Maybe they could sit this way forever.

A firecracker shot up like a missile. It slurped toward the sky, then exploded into one sharp, angry cackle.

Tink felt Alexis's arm slip away from hers as she stood up. "Coop!" Alexis called.

He made his way across the sand, and when he reached them, he leaned in for a kiss. Alexis let it brush one cheek, but Tink could see her smile, how it stayed plastered there, as she took his hand and curled into his chest.

"Hey." Coop nodded at Tink.

"Hey." Tink looked at the way his jeans stopped awkwardly at the tops of his too-white sneakers. She didn't know what Alexis saw in him. He was so quiet.

Len ran to them, breathless. "That was *my* cracker!" he shouted.

"That was crazy!" Kimmy landed right behind him.

"Try one," Len urged Tink.

Tink shook her head. "I don't know."

Alexis laughed against Coop's shoulder. "It's a rite of passage. Setting off firecrackers at Barnes Bluff."

"I'll get my hand blown off," Tink said.

"You won't," Alexis argued. "You light it. You run. It's no big deal, Tink. Really."

"Then why do it?" Tink asked.

Alexis rolled her eyes. "If you have to ask, you're already living a dead-end life. I can't help you."

Tink stood up and brushed off her shorts. "Okay."

Alexis arched her eyebrows up in surprise, then she softened. "It's fun. Right, Coop?"

He shrugged. "Sure."

"Come on." Len was already off and running, his legs and arms all skinny and wiry, into the night.

Tink followed with Kimmy yammering beside her. "It's like lighting a candle. You stand back, and then you just run."

"You haven't even done it," said Tink.

Kimmy groaned. "It's not like I haven't seen your dad do it a *thousand* times or anything."

Tink's dad was sorting through the box of crackers, and Tink marched up like she knew what she was doing. "So what do we have here?" she asked, not really sure why she was talking like a grandpa all of a sudden.

"Well, we've got some rockets." Her dad pulled out a skinny wooden stick with a rocket-shaped, rainbow-colored thingy on top.

"Can I shoot it?" she asked.

"Under my supervision."

"Okay." Tink wondered how hard it could be. It was just like lighting a birthday candle and running away from your wish.

"Let's find a good spot," her dad suggested.

"Where I did it," Len chimed in, pointing to a patch of crumpled sand and a bunch of sticks and wrappers left behind.

"Set it first," her dad instructed. He was always dripping in sweat, no matter the temperature, breathing in like he had to catch his last breath. "Point it toward the water. *Away* from you."

Tink knelt in the sand, set it pointing out toward the ocean, lit by all the porches of each beach house, which were strung like lanterns across the shore.

"We'll use these." He held out a box of long matches. They were the length of her forearm, and she pulled one out, realizing she'd never lit a match in her life, not even for a birthday candle.

But she knew about the chalky strip on the box, the way the tip caught fire, then simmered.

"Before you light it, test its stability." He tugged at the rocket, making sure it was stuck real good in the sand, then wiped the bottom of his shirt across his forehead. "Now just light it, blow out the match quick, and stand back." He pointed toward the beach grass, just beyond the house, and walked over there.

Tink held the box in one hand, the match in the other. She struck it a few times before it caught fire. Then she quickly lit the rocket, watching the snip of flame.

She blew out the match and ran.

She listened to the rocket's short whistle, her chest heaving. She turned back, looking for the trail of light, waiting for the cackle as it caught the wind and burst.

But she didn't see or hear any of it. Was it possible to have missed it, while turning her back?

Len whooped and Kimmy laughed.

Her dad ran his wrist across his sweaty cheeks. "Looks like you got yourself a dud, Tink."

She held the match in her clenched and clammy fist and looked at the rainbow rocket. It was face-first in the sand, smoldering. The waves settled closer and closer, until they lapped up the rainbow swirl and took it away.

LOW TIDE, 4:46 A.M.

I feel myself taken away with the tide. It opens up and swallows me, and I flail inside, coughing and sputtering. I'm shaken, stirred, then tossed. The sand scrapes my skin, and I claw at it but it slips away.

Then I open my eyes.

I'm not at the shore. It's not the Fourth of July. I'm not in the dream I dreamed. I'm in my bed, and it's sticky hot, and my stomach is aching.

HIGH TIDE, 11:41 A.M.

Later that morning, I sit at the edge of the deck stairs. They lead their way to the dunes, and I watch the beach grass sway. Seeing it, my heart catches. I feel like I'm back in my dreams.

But then I hear the shush of the sliding door, and the feeling passes. I remember I am where I am, where I've been for the past ten years, and I shake myself out of re-membering the dream. Soon Lindy's behind me, her hands at my shoulders. "You headed to Jeremiah's?" she asks.

"Yup," I say.

"Stop by the Shaky later," she tells me. That's what we call *the Shaky Docks*. I always eat there on Sundays. Lindy sneaks out clam strips, and we eat on the back steps during her break. "Elder'll be there," she says.

It jolts me. Sundays at the Shaky is *our* thing. Lindy's and mine.

"Okay?" she asks.

I nod fast, without thinking. "Okay."

Then I swallow hard and take off, wondering why she's got to pair me and Elder together all the time. Isn't it enough that I'm letting him into our house?

"See you later," she calls, and I can't even look back to wave.

The Shaky Docks was one of the first places Lindy took me after she found me. She tucked me in a booth sticky with ketchup. I fisted french fries, smashing them in my palms. I squeezed at Luss the line cook's scratchy, unshaven cheeks. Lindy said I didn't cry or fuss. I just fell into place, easy as the tides, a part of Barnes Bluff from day one.

When I get to Jeremiah's, Gramzy answers. The television's blazing, and Jeremiah gives me a chin nod, while the light from the TV bobs and dances around the room.

"Good, glad you're here." Gramzy's hands are wrinkled but soft as she takes my wrist. "I need a girl's opinion."

"On what?" I ask.

"Curtains," she says. "The boy's no use."

I follow her around the house, into the kitchen, where she stands with swatches of fabric against the pale yellow wall. "Bird's-eye or calico?" she asks, barely looking up at me. Then she pulls out a third. "There's also the pincheck, but I'm leaning away from it."

"I like flowers," I say. "Flowers are nice."

Gramzy looks me over. At the creases of my hands caked in dirt and my knees black from kneeling in sand. Living next to Lindy and me all these years, she should know there's nothing delicate about the two of us, nothing that knows the proper curtains for a home. Still, she smiles. "Flowers," she repeats, tasting the word on her tongue. "Calico it is." Then she repeats what she already told me. "The boy's no use for these kinds of things." She nods toward the living room. "Go on."

I guess she's done with me, so I jump the little step from the kitchen into the living room and collapse onto Gramzy's couch, which is covered in soft sheets because she's got a thing about keeping it *pristine*. Usually she's got the Home Shopping Network blaring at a supersonic volume, but Jeremiah's watching a boat sail around the ocean, his brow furrowed, all focused.

"Yoo-hoo, hello!" I shout.

"Oh, sorry." He fools with the remote. "I'm used to watching it at Gramzy levels."

"Whatcha watching?" I ask.

"Some National Geographic thing."

"What is it?"

"That old ship that sank. The *Titanic*. These scientists have all these tools to map the ocean. And they've got all this stuff they're finding on the ocean floor. See those twisting arrows?" He points at a map on the screen.

"The swirl?" I ask.

"Yup. They track the path of the wreckage, and then they know exactly the path it took before it sank."

The swirling arrows flash again.

"Pretty cool," I tell him. And it is, this idea of the ocean holding on to an entire history, revealing itself all these years later.

"Mm-hmm. Wanna see something?" he asks.

"Sure," I say.

He turns the television off. "We're going!" he calls out, not waiting to hear back from Gramzy, then he leads me outside, and we ramble over our sandy street, without saying a word. He takes me across the two-lane road, past the Beachcomber Motel, and on to the bay side, where the town gets its name. He holds up a shell, purple-spotted and shining. "It's a lady crab shell," he tells me. "They shed them as they get bigger and wait in the sand for a new one to grow." He hands it over. I feel how soft and glossy it is, how the little horns poke out, but they aren't sharp, just smooth, and rounded, left behind when the lady crab wanders out.

It's got to be something, doesn't it, to be able to leave the shell of yourself and walk away? "I'll keep one for the collection," I say.

Jeremiah nods, like he meant for that to happen all along.

I hold it in my hands and turn it over and around, inspecting it. "Do you know who lived in your house before you?" I ask.

"Gramzy, I guess."

"Before her?" I press.

He shakes his head. "It's hard to imagine anybody before Gramzy. Why?"

I shrug. "Just . . . I dreamed your house. I think . . ." I hesitate. I try to remember the details, the water, the shore, the house lit up, but all I can picture are shadows. The blur of people, their hair, maybe, but not their faces or names.

I wonder why this dream felt so full, why I still feel it in my gut every time I look at the water. It's like Tink's smoldering firecracker just landed right there. Maybe it did. I shake the feeling.

"You seen Turtle Lady?" he asks.

"Not since yesterday. You?"

"Nope," he says. "No turtles, either."

"I wonder where she keeps them. I wonder what else she's hiding in that house. I wonder—" I sigh. I wonder too much, maybe. I run my fingers over the lady crab shell. It's smooth and soft and cold. Then I get to wondering how long the lady crab waits for a shell that fits her and if the old shell tricks birds into thinking they've found something to eat.

"My dad's visiting," Jeremiah says out of nowhere.

I snap my head up, quick. "Your *dad*?"

He nods.

I'm about to say, *I didn't think you had one,* but of course he does. I know how kids are made, and it does take some kind of dad to get things going. I've got a dad, too, not one that I know, but he existed once or I wouldn't be here. "When's the last time you saw him?" I ask.

"He left when I was a baby."

I've never seen him with a dad. I just know about a mom who died of an infection right after he was born, and her mom, the Gramzy who runs the Pitch & Putt and sorts through fabric swatches for just the right curtains.

"Where does he live?" I ask.

He shrugs. "All over, I guess."

"What does he do?"

"He's all artsy or whatever. I guess he, like, *dabbles.* That's what Gramzy says."

I get this feeling Jeremiah doesn't know much.

"How long's he going to be here?" I ask.

"Don't know."

He breaks a dried stick of seaweed in half and matches the two pieces side by side. His voice gets quiet. "I don't want anything to change," he tells me.

I nod, fast, bobbing my head like a dumb bird. "Me either."

Jeremiah and I dilly around the rest of the day, collecting shells, skipping rocks across the bay, taking our bikes to the dirt road to see who's around and maybe see if Tanvi will let us take out the kayak from her parents' store.

Ted Light tails us for part of the afternoon. We've got ten-speeds, and he's still trolling around with his sister's old banana-seat bicycle that's called *Peaches & Cream*. Lindy's always telling me Ted "means well," but he doesn't brush his hair, he talks too much, and his idea of a good time is making up songs about going to space.

Still, there aren't too many of us poking about Barnes Bluff year-round, so I've gotten used to him.

By this time, we've come across Tanvi, who is sitting on her rickety old steps with a battered copy of some bodice-ripper romance book, which is nothing new, but she doesn't even look up when Jeremiah starts knocking on her head. "Yoo-hoo, anybody in there?"

She finally holds a finger up to us to wait a minute, mimes the words she's reading under her breath, then squashes the book against her legs. "My mom says I have to go outside and get some fresh air, and that is the *only* reason I'm out here, and it's as far as I'm going, so don't get all whiny about doing whatever it is you're going to be nagging me about in five seconds."

"We want to take the kayak out," Jeremiah says anyway.

"Pleeease." I clasp my hands together in prayer.

Tanvi doesn't look away from her book. "Do you see these steps?"

We nod.

"I'm not leaving them. It's stuffy out here, it's hot, and you know as well as I do if my mother didn't think I needed *fresh air* and an *education,* I'd never even leave my room."

Ted Light laughs, all snickery and high-pitched, and Tanvi's chin shoots up, finally taking us in, her cheeks turning flushed when she sees Ted Light hovering over his Peaches & Cream bike.

She's got a thing for him. She admitted it once. And while I acted like a five-year-old *ooh-la-la*-ing and singing about *Tanvi and Te-ed sitting in a tree,* she shut me down real quick, because it was much easier, she claimed, to end things before they began.

"But . . ." Jeremiah hesitates. "You've got a kayak."

Tanvi shoos her arm ahead, flustered. "It's all yours."

"Really?" I ask.

We hear Mrs. Ballard's unmistakable "Taaaaaaan-viiiii" bellow out onto the street from the back of the house, and then she's at the screen door. "Oh! Summer! Ted! Jeremiah!" she announces us. "Tanvi, when people are here, you invite them in, you do not make them linger on the front steps like dogs." Then she makes this kind of tsking noise and swings the door open.

Tanvi stands up quick. "They want to take the kayak out."

"Oh! Yes. Tanvi told you about the kayak, then. There was a mix-up on orders at the shop, so the seller reimbursed us for this. He said it's a Cadillac of kayaks, that's what he said, and we should embrace a life on the ocean, am I right, Tanvi?" She swirls her arms around in a circle, gesturing around the bay. "Then you'll all take it out?" She asks it like a question, but you can tell she means it like a command, especially when Tanvi holds out her book in protest. "I'm read—"

Mrs. Ballard removes the book from her hands. "If you are reading Tolstoy, Shakespeare, okay then, fine, we'll let you bury that nose of yours farther and farther into the book, of course, am I going to argue that? No, no, of course not. But *this* is not *that*." She makes her tsking noise again and reads the title out loud. *"Her Silent Thorn."* She sighs

50

and shakes the book out at us. Tanvi eyes Ted Light, and her face gets even more red. "This is for silly old ladies like me, Tanvi. Show them the kayak. Take the kayak. Show them."

Tanvi groans and gets all stompy up the steps. "Come on."

Jeremiah and I let our bicycles fall to their sides, so they're resting on the grass with the wheels circling in the breeze. Ted Light hesitates. "I've got piano lessons," he tells us.

"Well, there's only room for two of us, anyway," Jeremiah says, and I kick his shins.

"Next time," I say.

"I'm tackling the Chopin waltzes," Ted continues.

We nod.

"I'm *so* close to memorizing the *Minute* Waltz."

We continue nodding.

"If I memorize it, I get a sticker."

He kicks his heels in the dirt, and I get the feeling I get a lot around Ted, that he's always sticking around just one minute too long.

"I'll see you guys in school."

"Yup," I say.

Ted smiles. "Bye, Tanvi."

She doesn't respond, already leading us to the wrap-around porch, which is just like mine and Lindy's. It takes us to the dock in the backyard. Tanvi kicks at the pointy red kayak and wraps her arms around her chest. "Happy? It's a two-seater, so I'll *gladly* sit this one out."

She tosses out two life vests, faded from the sun. Then I watch her reach to the front of the kayak, where she pulls out an attached plastic box meant to keep your things dry. But, instead of a wallet and keys, there's a withered old paperback romance, and she flips to a page.

"You don't use a bookmark?" I ask. Since she always has her nose in a book, I never noticed.

"Nah." Then she plunks her hand to her head. "I file page numbers right here."

"How many books are you in the middle of this time?"

"Let's see." She looks up to the sky, thinking it out, counting under her breath.

"I've got one at the house, one in the kayak, one in the car, and at least two at school."

"Don't you get the stories confused?"

She rolls her eyes, like I'm talking crazy. "They're all different, Summer." Then she softens. "I'll loan you one if you want."

I reach out, turn the cover so I can see it. A bare-chested man with flowy hair and a woman with sleeves drooping to her elbows stand together in the rain. They're holding on to one another like if they let go, they'd die. *"Love's Tender Storm,"* I read out loud. Then I think of Lindy and Elder standing over our deck table with plasticky cheese and a bottle of smelly red wine. *Is that what love's like?*

I wonder. *Getting all stormed on?* "I don't know." I hesitate. "They sound kind of—"

"They're not dumb *or* silly," Tanvi chimes in before I can finish. "We have to embrace heroines who are willing to subvert the rules laid out for them and put their desires first," she huffs.

"I was going to say . . . sad. I don't know." I think back to the book Mrs. Ballard took away. *"Her Silent Thorn?* What does that even mean? How can a *thorn* be silent?"

"It's not about an *actual* thorn, Summer. Don't you know anything? It's about loving someone, *desperately"*— she clutches her hands to her chest—"but knowing they aren't good for you. And not to give anything away or anything . . . but . . . let's just say, no thorn stays silent, okay?"

I shrug. "Okay." I guess Elder is Lindy's thorn. I guess he just won't stay quiet anymore. I wish he would.

"A little help here, please?" Jeremiah scolds, trying to drag the kayak onto the dock with his skinny little arms.

I march over. "On three," I tell him, and we lift it up together, stepping across the planks of the dock toward the canal.

When we're stuffed like sausages into the life vests, we slip the kayak into the still waters, toss in the two-sided paddles, and scramble in after them until we're seated and ready.

"Now what?" I ask, my legs sticking out under the plastic point of the kayak, my feet all crunched.

"You don't know how to kayak?" Jeremiah asks.

I shake my head.

"Me neither."

"Tanvi!" we call together.

It takes her a little bit to slog over, her book out in front of her while she concentrates on the pages. She's perfected reading and walking, or so she's told me, but if she walked a little too far, she'd walk right off the dock. Knowing Tanvi, though, she'd just keep on reading, holding the book open up over her head.

"How do you move this thing?" I ask.

She drops her arm to her side and shakes her head. "You seriously don't know how to kayak?"

"Nope."

"I don't know," she says. "Move the paddles around or something."

Jeremiah plops one side of his paddle in the water.

"You have to do it together," she tells us.

I plop mine in and watch our paddles knock each other as we try to move.

She sighs. "In sync, geniuses."

We paddle in small circles around the dock. My arms are burning as we dizzy around, the two of us grunting and breathing and not saying much. We finally pick up some momentum. It feels like we're gliding.

I stop for a minute. I close my eyes and feel the freedom of moving while Jeremiah scurries his paddle.

When I open them up again, we're heading for the dock.

"Which way?" Jeremiah asks.

"Backwards!" I call out. But we're not fast enough. We just crash into the dock with a giant thud, and the kayak wobbles and tips, and before I know it, I'm sinking and paddling my arms, salt water rushing my insides.

I rise up coughing and take a huge breath, clothes and hair dragging me down as I grab hold of the dock and try to pull myself up.

Tanvi hasn't moved. Her legs are pretzeled together, hair lopping over the pages. She's absorbed in the story of two people trying to stay in love through a storm.

LOW TIDE, 5:32 P.M.

I bike up to the Shaky. Even though we tried to dry off in the sun all afternoon, I'm still a little damp from our fall in the water. My arms feel tired from paddling the kayak around. The dock's full, and a few people are standing at the order window, waiting for fish fry. I circle to the back, where the dumpsters are piled high with garbage, and I lean my bike up against the paint-peeled railing of the back stairs.

Through the kitchen, it's flaming hot, smelling of fried everything. It's clanking with all kinds of pots and pans. Coffee cup saucers skid and plates slap against the counter. As I slip on through, I hear Lindy's voice above it all as she shouts orders. Luss nods his chin at me while he flips crab cakes. Silverware echoes in the sink basin.

I imagine Luss shucking oysters at the bar, tossing half shells on iced platters while the rest collect in giant

Tupperware bins. Lindy used to bring me buckets of the leftovers, but there are only so many gnarly and barnacled oyster shells you can dig through before it's all just more and more of the same.

I push through the swinging door and nearly clip a red-faced Lindy as she spins toward me, carrying plates that line up her arms. "Luss!" she shouts. "I'm going on break in five!" Then she tips her chin at me. "I'll meet you out back."

When I get out there, Elder's sitting at the lopsided picnic table, and he hops up when he sees me, slamming his knee against the wood, then pretending it doesn't hurt him. "Summer!" He tries to smile between grimaces.

At least the rat dog's not here, but I can't help looking toward the kitchen, wishing Lindy's *five* would turn into zero.

There's no escape.

I take my time going down the steps and lift up my bicycle. I actually use the kickstand this time, then I lean against the frame like it's a seat.

"So. Shells," he starts.

Here we go.

"What's the fascination?"

I shrug. "They're pretty. They're the same and, also, different." I don't know how to explain. It began with my shell necklace and Lindy and me walking up and down the shore with buckets, collecting as many as we could for me to string them into more necklaces to sell on the beach.

Then it turned into protecting the most beautiful of them for me, lining them up along the windowsills, until there were too many to count. Lindy joked that I'd bring the shore indoors, a never-ending beach. She helped me store them. She helped me keep the shells the sea had captured and polished and set free. Together, we took them, before the ocean could take them again.

"You guys must have thousands," he tells me, bobbing his head, nodding like he's never talked about anything more interesting.

"Mm-hmm."

"So, thanks," he starts in.

"For what?"

"For agreeing to let me move in. My apartment is much too small for the three of us. It just makes sense, with the space you have."

Nothing will change, Lindy said, but how could it not?

"I make a mean Bolognese," he says, out of nowhere.

Bolognese? I wonder what he's talking about.

"So you and Lindy have been here, what? Ten years?" he asks.

"I've been here ten years. She's been here a little longer."

"She doesn't talk about family much."

"*I'm* her family," I argue.

"Well, right, but she's got a mom, in Delaware, or something?"

I nod. "We visited her once." I remember the spare

kitchen, two cups of coffee, an orange juice for me. The bathroom smelled like powder, and there was a big yellow bottle of something called AFTER BATH SPLASH by Jean Naté. There were no photographs on the walls or shelves. "But they don't get along."

"How come?"

I kick my sneakers in the sand and mash it around. I don't actually know. Lindy always says she's moved on from Delaware, from that life. I make up an answer. "Artistic differences." It seems like something Lindy would say.

Elder laughs. "I don't think that's what you mean."

"That's exactly what I mean." I dig my heel, watching the sand glide to the ground.

"Why did she pick this place?"

"Why don't you ask *her* that?"

"She's got a way of ignoring those kinds of questions."

"Maybe she doesn't want you to know," I say.

I can tell he doesn't like the idea. His eyes do this thing like they don't know where to look. The truth is, Lindy doesn't answer questions like that. She waves them away like you would a fly.

"Lindy's great," he tells me. "I've never met anyone like her."

I resist the urge to roll my eyes.

"Most people I know, my age, anyway, they don't have twelve-year-olds," he says. "I mean, I don't know a lot of twelve-year-olds. I mean, it's fine. It's just. Different."

"Okay . . ."

"I guess I don't really understand . . . why . . ." He's looking for words. "Why she'd do something like that. You were so . . . little. And she was only twenty. It seems, I don't know, hard. Unnecessarily hard."

He watches my reaction, but I'm not sure what he wants me to say. That it would have been easier without me? That she should have left me behind, gone her own way, so we wouldn't end up here today?

It's not like I don't know. I'm *hers*, but I'm not. Not really. And I know that will never change.

I remember when Elder and I first met, before Lindy told him I was adopted. He stood at the doorway, looking behind me, to Lindy, who stood with her hands on my shoulders, presenting me like I was an open gift he would have to return. He looked from Lindy to me and back again, and I could tell he couldn't understand how we were related. Everybody else in Barnes Bluff knows about me landing here, but Elder didn't. He couldn't. The way he looked back and forth, confused, it made me wish that Lindy and I looked more alike so he didn't have to question it. It made me wish that anyone who didn't know us wouldn't have to wonder.

I tell him what he wants to hear. "I guess she should have left me there."

"Oh. Oh. *No.* That's not what I meant. Of course not."

"I guess that's what *you* would have done," I continue.

"I don't . . . I mean . . ." He speaks slow, deliberate. "You're *right*, but—"

The back door slams, and Lindy asks, "Right about what?"

Elder's eyes are big and confused. I spring up from my bike, and it falls backward.

I scramble to pick up my bike while she looks between us. "So serious." Then she laughs. She holds a plastic tray with cardboard plates of oysters, peel-and-eat shrimp, and, my favorite, clam strips with tartar sauce.

I figure I might as well lay it bare. "We were talking about me—"

"And shells," Elder chimes in, fast. "Their variety."

"Her collection is solid. A little out of control. But beautiful." She holds the tray out to me. "Right?"

I nod and grab my clam strips, then take up my post against my bike. When I take a bite of a clam strip, I nearly gag. My belly feels sick with the seawater I swallowed.

Lindy slips onto the bench next to Elder. Not across from him, the way two people are supposed to sit when they eat a meal together, but squeezing as close as possible, leaving nothing but an empty space on the other side.

She hands him the oysters. "Your favorite. Montauk Pearls."

He grins his goofy grin, and his bony knees hit the table. I watch him, knowing now, at least, where he stands.

On the side of not wanting anything to do with me.

Later that night, I stretch the sleeves of my hoodie to the tips of my fingers and rest my head against a wooden lounge chair on the back porch, listening for the sound of Elder's truck. I try to savor the last nights of summer, but it's already too cold. The air smells salty and wet. The stars stay hidden behind the clouds. I can barely hear the ocean over the blowing wind.

Elder's truck roars, and the lights from his high beams swish across the beach grass. I hear the motor run and a door slam. The lights linger a few moments too long, while Lindy's boots clamor up the front steps. As soon as the screen door bangs closed, I clutch the ends of my sweatshirt and watch the lights back away.

Lindy calls my name.

I mumble, "Out here!"

Soon she's a blurred outline behind the screen. "What

are you doing out there in the dark?" She flicks the porch light on.

Then she joins me, pulling a deck chair up. She doesn't look cold, not with her leather bomber jacket zipped tight and her knitted fingerless gloves scrunched at her wrists.

She *should* stick out like a sore thumb in Barnes Bluff, but instead, she's woven tight to the thread of this place. We both are.

I curl up in my chair, trying to stay warm. Before I know it, the leaves will fall, they'll harvest pumpkins on the North Fork, and winter will nose its way in.

"How was the rest of your shift?" I ask.

"Uneventful."

"Elder stayed?" I ask.

"Mm-hmm."

It comes out harsher than I want it to. "I like Sundays being *our* day at the Shaky."

"Oh. Okay." I watch the recognition race through her. "Of course. I'm sorry."

It bothers me that it didn't even occur to her I'd want to keep it that way. Then more things start gnawing at me. I sit up quick. "Why'd you leave it up to me, anyhow?" I ask.

"Leave what up to you?"

"The whole Elder-moving-in thing."

"I want you to be comfortable with it, Summer. I thought you should have a say."

"So if I say *no,* you'll change your mind?" I ask.

She hesitates.

I fall back into my chair. "Didn't think so."

I can't think of a time when Lindy and I weren't on the same page. *Why is it happening now?*

"I thought we could ease into it," she says. "I thought we'd start with Sundays at the Shaky first. I don't know. I'm new at this."

She edges closer to me, tugs at the paws of my sweatshirt covering my palms. "I don't want you to feel left out," she says. "I know what that's like."

"You do?"

"I was always the one left behind. Always the third wheel. Blech."

"In school?" I wonder.

"Just . . . in life." She goes *vague,* what Mrs. Grady says when we're not specific enough in our convictions.

She rests her hand at my wrist and says, "Sundays at the Shaky are *ours.*"

"Okay. Good."

But it doesn't feel like enough. I want all of Lindy, not one place or one day.

She stands up, pulling my hand with her. "Come on. It's late. And it's freezing out here."

I trudge behind her. She flicks the porch light out, and we're left in darkness, feeling our way through the house I've lived in ever since I can remember. When she found me, when she let me into her life, I wonder if she knew she'd have to break us open someday to let others in.

Lindy leaves me at the foot of my unmade bed. She kisses my forehead with a whispered *good night,* and I collapse onto the crumpled sheets, my arms sore from kayaking, my stomach aching with salt and seawater and clam strips. I bunch my hands underneath me because even if they get tingly and fall asleep themselves, it makes me feel safe.

I leave the window open, holding on to the last gasps of summer breeze. I shut my eyes and drift closer to sleep.

HIGH TIDE, 11:40 P.M.

Tink squirted mustard on her hot dog. She eyed Kimmy, who was scooting her deck chair closer to Len. Tink hated the fact that it used to be the three of them together and now it was all disjointed and weird.

Tink's mom slid past her, leaving the musky waft of her perfume behind. She wrapped one arm around Kimmy's shoulders as she reached over her to grab a bun from a flimsy plastic platter. She was affectionate like that, always pressing wet kisses on Tink's cheeks, crushing her in suffocating hugs, and Tink secretly liked it even if she knew she wasn't supposed to. She was supposed to roll her eyes and *Mo-om* her.

But Kimmy didn't brush her aside the way she would her own mother. In fact, she seemed kind of happy in the embrace even as Tink's mom lingered too long in it.

"What're you all doing today?" her mom asked. "I heard about this new go-kart place."

"Sounds cool," Tink said.

Kimmy frowned. "I'd rather go to the beach."

Tink held back a groan. She didn't want to go to the beach again and lie out on towels the way Kimmy did, making sure she tanned evenly as she read celebrity gossip magazines.

"What about you, Len?" Tink's mom asked.

"Sure," he said, shoving a hot dog in his mouth. "Go-karting sounds fun."

"Well, maybe I'd check it out," Kimmy said quickly.

As soon as she agreed, Tink lost interest. "Maybe tomorrow," she murmured.

Tink's mom looked between them, suspicious, and Tink wondered how she always knew when something was up.

"Didn't you all talk about doing that sandcastle competition again this year?" her mom asked. "Isn't that coming up?"

Tink brightened. "Oh yeah!"

"I don't know. It was kind of lame," Kimmy said.

Tink didn't know what she wanted—for Kimmy to *want* to do the same things Tink did or for her to *not* want to do them. It seemed whichever way it went, it made her angry.

"I'm going to take a walk," Tink said, holding on to her hot dog.

"A walk where?" Len called, and maybe there was a little desperation in his tone, if she thought about it?

Her mom followed as Tink skipped down the first set of deck steps. "What's up with you and Kimmy?"

"Nothing," Tink said, her voice as flat as possible, making her way, fast, across the wraparound porch, in between bites of her hot dog.

But then she stopped. She was tired of holding everything in. "We're just not into the same things anymore."

"Mmm. I worried that would happen."

Tink swallowed hard. "You did?"

"I don't know. Kimmy's always been more advanced. Your sister was like that. It was exhausting. It still is."

Tink nodded. It *was* exhausting.

"You're a late bloomer, like I was."

Tink flushed. "God, Mom."

"It's true! But it all evens out, eventually."

Tink nodded, wishing it would even out faster. It felt like everyone—her family, her friends, the kids at school—they were all out of sync. "I'm walking to the bay side," Tink said, and her mom grazed her lips across Tink's forehead in a fast kiss. "Be careful."

Tink climbed down the tall wooden steps toward the front of the house, skipping along the sandy dirt road, kicking up dust like a wild horse.

By the time she turned the corner, crossing closer to the bay side of Barnes Bluff, Len was huffing and puffing right next to her, wiping sweat from his upper lip. "Where ya going?" he asked.

She got herself ready for Kimmy's inevitable giggling behind them. But, when she turned around, it was just the road, lined with beach grass, and Len shuffling his giant bare feet beside her.

"I'm—" *Sick of Kimmy,* she thought to say but held it at her tongue. She stuffed the last bit of hot dog in her mouth and spoke all garbled. "I'm bored."

"Me too," Len agreed.

She stopped. "Where's Kimmy?" she asked.

He shrugged. "Took off before she could catch up, I guess."

Tink smirked.

Len let a little laugh bubble from his lips and caught himself.

"It's hot," she went on. "But I don't even feel like swimming."

"We could hang out where Alexis works, maybe?" Len suggested.

"Alexis doesn't want me there," she murmured.

"So? Who died and left her queen?"

Tink almost smiled.

"We could hang with Coop?" he said. "He's always at the marsh."

She scrunched her nose. "*Coop?*"

"What? He's cool."

She had to admit she was curious about this kid that Alexis was spending all her time with, who stood at Alexis's side and said not much more than *hey*.

"All right."

They walked to the line of trees that stretched along the narrow waterway toward the marsh, where a collection of old canoes and boats sat soaking in leftover rain.

"Hey, Coop!" Len called, sloshing through the mud. Tink followed. She listened to the slopping sound and eyed the mess of paddles, ropes, and discarded boats.

Coop didn't look up. He sat hunched over the underside of a canoe. She could see paints and spray bottles nestled on the ground.

Len marched up to him, and Tink ran her gaze across the entire length of the canoe. It was covered in delicate, purposeful brushstrokes, a jumbled but detailed painting of an enormous menagerie. The creatures were so vivid, it looked like a photo.

Tink stood gaping. "*You* did this?"

Coop finally looked up, his eyes sharper than she'd seen them all summer, like he was in his element for once. "No one uses the boats, so I thought, why not?"

Tink stared at the animalscape. Birds in flight. A tiger. A kangaroo with a lopsided, wicked smile. There were mythical creatures, centaurs and three-eyed dogs and fish-tailed lions. Falling flower petals covered the spaces in between. It looked like a lot of work, and he seemed to be filling in every inch of blank space.

"Wow," Len chimed in.

Coop rested his paintbrush against the side of the boat and reached into the pocket of his flannel shirt. "Cigarette?"

Tink shook her head no, real fast.

Len sat down beside him. "Sure."

Tink's eyes grew wide, watching as Coop patted his pocket. He handed over a cigarette and lighter to Len.

Len handled the lighter with two hands, like he was swinging a tennis racket. Somehow, he got it going, the cigarette kind of drooping from his lips as the lighter twitched and lit a flame.

Tink leaned against a tree.

"We're bored," Len confessed.

"That's Barnes Bluff for you." Coop's voice was soft. "Where's Kimmy?"

Len shrugged. "At the house, I guess."

"She still crazy over you?" Coop asked.

"Yeah," Len said, like it was nothing.

Tink couldn't believe it, with the way Kimmy had made her crush on Len into the biggest of all *big* deals, making her promise and swear on imaginary Bibles that she'd take it to her grave and never tell a living soul.

Now here they were in the middle of the marsh, Coop

and Len blowing smoke into the air like it didn't matter at all.

She slid down the tree and curled her bare legs under her butt.

It must be nice, she thought, *to be a boy.*

"So what's with the animals?" she asked Coop.

"Just painting as many as I can think of."

"They'd destroy one another," she said. "If it were real."

Coop looked at her, maybe for the first time ever, and smiled for the slightest second. "Yeah, well it's not."

She scanned the rainbow of color. "Do you have a turtle?" she wondered out loud. It was the first animal she thought of. One lucky enough to be able to hide inside of itself.

Coop took a long drag of the cigarette and looked down at his own work. "I guess not."

LOW TIDE, 5:26 A.M.

The ocean sweeps up and over me. Seaweed slithers across my arms, and I feel the fish nip at my toes. My chest stiffens and stings. I can't breathe, but I can see the water swirling all around. It fills my lungs and loses itself inside me. Then I hit the sand with a thud.

I wake with a start. I'm not in the ocean. I'm not at the marsh. I'm nestled with the old flowered sheets, and my hair is sliding down a lumpy pillow, and Coop and Tink and Len are all gone.

Or I am.

It's hard to tell which is true.

I feel for the dream inside me. Instead of pulsing in my memory, it feels as if it's trapped in my gut, and I hold my belly, feeling sick and strange. *What's there?* I wonder. *That leads me here?*

I don't know.

But I *know* something about this dream. Something about it feels like it's a part of me. I sit up and bunch the sheets to the bottom of the bed. Through the window, I can see the pink of the morning, just rising up.

I know that marsh. And I need to get to it.

If I leave now, I can get there and back before school.

leave a note for Lindy and slip out the door, as quiet as I can. The morning takes big, wide yawns in the hazy sky. I lift my bike from where it's sprawled out on the front lawn and take off, pedaling fast. My tires trail through the loose sand.

With nobody out, Barnes Bluff looks like a skeleton of itself. Nothing but tickly beach grass, the salty smell of the ocean, and a stale whiff of bay. All the houses blend into the white sky, and I cross over Main Street, past the church, the post office, and Quigley's Pub, which has the best cheeseburgers in town. It's not like the fried fish at the Shaky, but it's as good as it gets around here.

I cross to the bay side and feel the dream start to drift from my memory. I don't remember Tink's and Len's footsteps anymore. The sound of their voices is gone. But I know the marshland that leads to the landing. I know where everyone leaves their old paddleboats. It's the kind of place that's just on the way to somewhere else.

I take a curve onto the main road.

When I see the marsh ahead, I have to get over the metal railing, so I toss my bike first, then I hop over and step through the pools of water and sand.

The boats are there. Some of them collect water in their hulls, and, I realize, if I'm going to find what I'm looking for, I'm going to have to overturn them all.

There are about two dozen or so boats, and as the dream fades, I can't remember the exact kind or color I saw.

I send the boats toppling over and scan their deep-welled bottoms. Then I find it, next to some old soda cans.

The boat.

Coop's boat.

Round-bottomed and covered in faded paint.

I run my fingers across the smooth wood. There's a date carved into it: *July 31st, 2001.* There's a painted turtle, with its little head poking out. I smile.

Just like I dreamed, it's a full mosaic of animals. I'm seeing them just the way Tink and Len did.

Something in me knew I would, but the truth still knocks me in the chest. I place my hand there, like I've got to trap it.

I'm dreaming something real.

It's then I hear a slopping sound behind me, and I turn around to find muddy rubber boots, thick calves, a flowery muumuu dress, and that big old gauzy bun at the top of her head.

Turtle Lady.

It's the closest I've ever been to her watchful eyes and those thin lips, which push out a grunt. Her voice is rough and fast. "Watch your step."

My voice fails me.

Her hands are at her hips and she's shaking her head, back and forth. "Quit disturbing things. Go on," she demands. "Quit nosing around. Let it be."

Let *what* be?

But like I've grown accustomed to doing with Turtle Lady, I run away before I can say a thing.

HIGH TIDE, 12:18 P.M.

The lunchroom is all loud and echoey as I slap my tray against the table, a bunch of conversations mixing with the smell of smoky grill. Tanvi's got her nose stuffed in a book, no surprise there, except she's got a cloth cover so nobody knows she's reading some blazing bodice ripper.

I've got whatever the cafeteria dude slops onto my tray with his rubber gloves and a ladle, because when Lindy leaves the Shaky, she wants nothing to do with cooking, ever. I run my spoon through the lumps, thinking it might be chili. Jeremiah eats a bagged lunch from Gramzy, which means a cheese and mustard sandwich, an apple he throws in the garbage, and a juice box like he's five. It's the first time I've seen him all day, and I can't wait to tell him about Turtle Lady.

"I went to the marsh this morning," I tell him.

"I'm reeeading," Tanvi singsongs, like we're just

supposed to sit here in silence while she devours entire romances.

Jeremiah ignores her. "What marsh?"

I guess when you live between an ocean and a bay, that's a fair question. "The one past Main, on the bay side, where all the old paddleboats are."

Jeremiah doesn't look impressed. "Oh. So?"

"Turtle Lady," I say.

Jeremiah's eyes widen. "At the marsh?"

"At the marsh."

He crams the sandwich into his mouth. "What's she doing there?"

"Telling me not to *disturb things*," I say. "To watch my step."

"Wait, wait, wait, back up," Jeremiah says between chews. "*Disturb* things? What were *you* doing there?"

"So . . . remember how I dreamed your house?"

"Yeah."

"Well, the dreams are getting, I dunno, more and more involved, I guess. More and more . . . *real*. Like—" I try to explain before getting interrupted.

"This seat open?" It's Ted Light, holding a tray at his waist.

"I guess," I say at the same time Tanvi yelps just a little too loud, "No."

Ted looks toward Jeremiah, like he might be the deciding factor, and Jeremiah shrugs a bit. "Why not?"

Tanvi sighs loudly and brings her book a little closer to her face, but Ted Light doesn't seem bothered, the tray resting on the pudge of his tummy as he slides in next to Tanvi and immediately begins asking questions. "What are you talking about?"

"Dreams," I say.

"Like aspirations or the kind you have when you fall asleep?" He shoves a spoonful of the unidentifiable slop into his mouth.

"The sleep kind," says Jeremiah.

"I dream piano pieces," he tells us, and he drops his spoon and lifts his hands up, fingering something in the air, like he's hammering out notes on a floating piano. They match a buzzing hum from his lips. It's weird but also mesmerizing. I even see Tanvi peek out from behind her book.

"Once I dreamed a whole piece I'd been trying to get right. Dreamed it from beginning to end. I woke up and ran to the piano and tried to pick it up from there. Nothing but nonsense." He laughs and shakes his head, letting his fingers fall back to his spoon. "I forgot ketchup. It makes everything better. Can I get you anything?" He looks at the three of us.

Jeremiah and I shake our heads. Tanvi is silent. Ted Light shrugs and takes off for his ketchup.

"What's this all about?" I ask Tanvi.

"What's what about?" she asks.

"It's just Ted. You don't have to be such a scrooge about him. You like him. He might like you. I don't understand."

"He's inconvenient," she says. "End of story."

I'm about to question her when Ted Light slides in with his ketchup packets, ripping them open, one after the other. His hand motions are graceful, even as he's glopping ketchup into his bowl.

"So, what's this about dreams?" he asks.

"I dreamed about this old canoe with a painting on it," I explain. "In the marsh. And then I went to the marsh and it was there. Exactly as I saw it in my dream."

"And Turtle Lady doesn't want you messing with it?" Jeremiah raises his eyebrows.

"Bingo."

"Weird."

Tanvi places her book on the table. "How do you know you didn't see this canoe first and then dream it? And then see it again?"

"I thought you were reading?" I ask.

"I was. Doesn't mean I'm not listening. It takes a high level of cognitive ability to be able to follow two separate narratives at the exact same time. I can."

Jeremiah grunts.

"Well, I know I've never seen it before," I tell her.

"But how do you *know* know? I mean, you could have

seen it and buried the memory deep in your subconscious, only to have it come out when you're letting your guard down, for example, in your sleep."

"But I've never—"

"*Or*, someone could have told you about it. That's possible, right?"

"I guess—"

"Dreams are born from what's real."

"How do you know?" I ask.

"I read a book once, about this Freudian psychologist and his patient who became his lover, and he was trying to interpret her dreams, and then he learned she was dreaming about him, and let's just say, the things she was dreaming were *not* good, and it got really messy for a while, but in the end, he put her under hypnosis and found out she was *really* channeling her frustration with an old lover into their relationship, and the dreams had nothing to do with him at all, so they were able to put aside everything and fall in love."

I groan. "What does that have to do with *anything*?"

"Wait. Where was I going with this?" She looks to Jeremiah, who turns the smooth red apple in his hands and shrugs.

"Beats me." He takes aim for the garbage pail and tosses the apple right in. "But you'd think someone with a *high level of cognitive ability* would know."

Tanvi scowls.

"You're saying that dreams come from real desires. Real thoughts. Real feelings," Ted chimes in, his mouth full of his ketchup concoction. "Right?"

Tanvi nods. "Right."

"What do you think the dreams are about?" Ted asks me, his stare intent, like he has to have an answer.

I think of Tink again. It's like I know her without *knowing* her. She's someone to me. I think of the year. 2001. Long before I even existed. I think of Turtle Lady telling me to watch my step. Could she have something to do with these dreams?

"I don't know." I sigh. "Any of you know a Len?" I ask. "He'd be our parents' age. Hypothetically."

"Len like Leonard?" Tanvi asks.

"I guess."

They all shake their heads.

"Alexis? Kimmy . . ." I hesitate and feel my face go red as they stare. "It's just . . . the dreams. They feel like they happened once."

Tanvi sighs melodramatically. "I hear you." She picks up her book. "We all need an escape."

"Maybe," I say quietly. Is that what it is? An escape? From the mess with Lindy and Elder? From mold-less bread and a whole school year before summer comes again?

I try to think about where I might have seen that boat. Like Tanvi and Ted said, maybe I'm dreaming something

I've already seen, rather than the other way around. I take a bite of the warm mush. It's vaguely beefy. It's neither terrible nor good, just in the middle, like everything that comes from the school kitchen.

"Hey, Jeremiah, your Gramzy keeps records, right?" Ted asks.

"Of what?"

"At the Pitch & Putt. You know how you've got to sign in to rent clubs or play in the game room? Maybe your dream people, or whoever, were there."

I let myself smile. "That's genius."

Ted smirks and taps his head with his finger, looking right at Tanvi. "High level of cognitive ability."

Tanvi slumps behind her book and shakes her head, but I see her mouth turn up into an amused smile.

After school, we ride our bikes home to Jeremiah's, tossing them up against the old shack of the Pitch & Putt. The screen door creaks, and Jeremiah calls out for Gramzy. Jeremiah grazes his fingers along the kitchen counter for food, then he offers up a granola bar, which he tosses into my hand before I can refuse.

He tears into his bar, crumpling the wrapper and speaking in between chomps. "Gramzy!" he calls out again, and I follow him through the bright kitchen to the living room, with its heavy drapes and paisley couch, a thick rug, and old-lady knickknacks everywhere.

Instead of Gramzy, we see a tall man stand up from the couch, real quick, his eyes huge, his legs and arms all dangly, like he's this wiggly basketball player jamming across the court. I recognize him right away, with the way he stands in his tan blazer. Up close I can see the notebook poking out of the pocket, thick with scribbles. He's the stranger I saw standing on the boardwalk a few days ago. I can see that he is all Jeremiah, or Jeremiah's all him, whichever way it goes, with wild hair and heavy eyes and the same calm smile.

I stand back as Jeremiah stands rigid, and I get the feeling this man's going to swoop in for an unwanted hug just as Gramzy's coming from the other room, her voice as no-nonsense as always. "Jeremiah. This is your father."

I expect Jeremiah's eyes to go wild or something, but instead they go dead, this glazed look across his face, like I could wave a wand in front of it and not even get the slightest reaction. I feel a little sick inside, knowing I shouldn't be here for this big reunion, and I start backing toward the kitchen, when I see Gramzy wave her hand over, beckoning me in, and it's clear we're trapped in this room, all four of us in a minor hostage situation.

Maybe Jeremiah's dad gets his cue from the dead look in Jeremiah's eyes, because he doesn't go for the hug I thought he would. He holds out his hand for a shake. Jeremiah doesn't move, and I think of nudging him over.

"This is Summer," Gramzy announces, and I wonder if I should curtsy or something, everything feels so weirdly formal. Instead, I reach out for his extended hand and immediately regret it. He didn't mean it for me.

His hands are callused and his fingers are wiry-long, wrapping themselves around the back of my hand. It's a bit of a limp handshake, unsure, awkward, not like Lindy taught me, to shake a hand like I *mean* it.

"I live next door," I tell him. "And I'll be getting back right now. Right now," I repeat.

Jeremiah doesn't move, but it's like he snaps back into life. "Gramzy, I need your records. Your summer records."

Gramzy eyes me.

"Not *that* Summer. The summer records for the Pitch & Putt."

"What on earth for?" she wonders. "Your father's here."

"We need to see who's been coming through. Summer's been dreaming about a bunch of kids, and we need to know if they're real and stuff."

Gramzy looks at me for an explanation, and I shrug. There's no other way to explain it, is there? Weirdo Summer needs to know if her dream people are real or not.

"They're behind the desk. This isn't the CIA."

Jeremiah turns around and marches back through the kitchen toward the Pitch & Putt hut. His dad looks as confused as I do.

"Nice to meet you, sir," I say. And, this time, I do curtsy, then walk off behind Jeremiah. Just before I leave the room, I hear Gramzy say, "I don't know what you're expecting after twelve years. Your very own coronation? He'll come around when he wants to. That's his right."

As I slip out the screen door to the hut, I see Jeremiah crouching behind the desk, pulling out a thick black binder. I'm about to pounce, *What was that?* But something stops me. If, after all these years, I came across a dad I never knew was mine, and I was the nonconfrontational Jeremiah I knew, I'd probably turn right back around, too.

He plops the binder on the desk and pushes it toward me. "Here."

I nod and walk toward the book. Jeremiah stands stiff, hands in his pockets, unsure of where to go next. I can tell he doesn't know what might be there for him, inside where his dad is, or outside, or maybe anywhere.

I turn to the first page, toward Gramzy's neat, loopy writing. It's like a page from the cursive-writing handbooks you get in third grade. The names are in neat little rows along with the day and time they checked in.

The binder's thick and it spans years.

"Scan it with me," I urge him. "I'm looking for a Len, an Alexis, a Kimmy, or a Tink."

"Tink?"

I shrug.

He leans over my shoulder.

I see some kids' names from school. Gum-snapping Langston Cross. Willis Walker and her snot-nosed little sister. Darren Ledbetter, who comes almost every single day from June to September. My name doesn't come up. I play Pitch & Putt for free.

I turn back as far as I can, to the very beginning. I look at the year. 2009.

I sigh.

"What?" Jeremiah asks.

"It's just ten years ago."

"What's that got to do with anything?"

"The boat was made in 2001."

Jeremiah's brow furrows. I can tell he's trying to figure it all out. "Do you remember what they look like?"

I close my eyes, the memory of their faces blank. I shake my head. "Some things are crystal clear. Some things are all blurry."

"That's dreams for ya."

I sigh. "Yeah."

"Well, what's making them happen? Where are they coming from?"

I think about the way it felt like they were in my stomach. "It's almost like I swallowed them," I say with a laugh.

But then I stop myself. Maybe it's not so funny. Each dream ended with *me* inside the ocean. With the *ocean* inside me. That sick feeling each morning. It was salt water. Sitting in me. First from the riptide. Then from the kayak tipping over.

"The ocean," I whisper. My heart beats a little faster as I let the idea take hold, and then I say it firm. "It's coming from the ocean. I swallowed a whole bunch of ocean. Twice."

Jeremiah doesn't question it, just lets his eyes grow wide. "And the ocean is where you got your start," he states, like he's mulling it over.

"Maybe they've got to do with *me*. With where I came from. I mean, they're *inside* me for a reason, right?"

"A part of your subconscious. Like Tanvi was saying."

"Mm-hmm. All I've got in my life is an *after*. I've never known the *before*."

"And this dream . . ." Jeremiah pieces it all together. "Is part of your *before*?"

"Maybe?"

It's making some sense. An idea snags at my heart. It's quick. But it's there. A hypothesis. To whatever this science experiment is.

My mother.

I've let snippets of who she might be and what she might look like creep in and out of my mind over the years. Long dark hair that might match mine. A laugh that's bigger or brighter than mine could ever be. A love of the ocean and stars. Maybe these dreams are letting me get closer to knowing her.

"Well, whatever it is, it's leading me to places Turtle Lady doesn't think I should be snooping around in," I say.

"Do you think she knows something?" Jeremiah asks.

I let the thought sit with me. Is it possible my story is tied up with hers? "I mean, she *is* the only person in Barnes Bluff nobody knows much about."

"A little like you."

A little like me.

"See this?" Jeremiah leans in and puckers his lips together. "Smacked my lip on the corner of the sandbox," he says. "I bled straight through to Gramzy's shirt." He tugs at his puffy pink bottom lip. "You see the scar?"

I sit up, lean in, and see a jagged little white line stretching to his chin.

"I was two," he says.

"And you remember it?"

"Yup. Mrs. Grady says it's easy to remember messed-up events."

"Okay. What's that got to do with anything?" I wonder.

"Getting plucked from the ocean and ending up in Lindy's backyard would be a pretty memorable event."

"Yeah. You would think."

"Maybe these dreams will lead to a memory," he says. "You just need to dig it up."

I smile, thankful that whoever dropped me here in Barnes Bluff dropped me next to Jeremiah Cooper.

"He's not what I expected," he says, quiet.

At first, I wonder what he means, then I realize he's

talking about his dad, the gangly dude in Gramzy's knick-knacked living room.

He wanders away from the binder and plunks himself on the flowery couch. Dust rises in clouds of pillowy smoke. Then he sighs. "There's too much to sort out."

"He seems like he could be nice?" I ask it like a question.

"Maybe. I just wish I knew what he was doing here, ya know? After all this time, I mean, am I supposed to jump in his arms and call him *Daddy*?"

I shake my head. "Let Gramzy sort it all out. I mean, she's not *his* mom. She's not going to leave you high and dry."

"I don't want him here. I like things the way they are."

I'm about to say, *Nothing has to change,* but stop myself. When a person waltzes into your life after twelve years, it has a way of complicating things. Like Elder walking into the Shaky and sweeping Lindy off her tired feet. Like a story unfolding in your dreams for the first time, making you question what's real and what's not. I want to tell him everything will be okay, but I don't know that, so I grab on to what I do know.

"He's here to see you," I tell him. "For whatever reason. That's a nice thing. That's more than my parents, whoever they are, have ever done for me."

Jeremiah doesn't look up, fiddles with his fishhooks.

"I guess, in some ways, it feels like, if *he's* here, then *she* should be here."

I know what he means without him having to explain. "Your mom."

He nods. "I always knew *he* was out there. Somewhere, at least. But she'll never be . . . *anywhere.*"

I swallow hard. For once, I think I'm lucky. There's still a possibility my own mother could turn up here, just like Jeremiah's dad.

He sighs. "What am I supposed to say to him?"

I shrug. "I dunno. Let *him* do the talking." Then I think about what *I* would want, if a mom and dad showed up in our mismatched living room, stood up from the couch, held out their hands for a limp shake. "Ask him to tell you who you were."

"When?" Jeremiah asks, confused.

"*Then,*" I say. "When you were brand-new." His fish-hooks quietly chime against one another, like he's strumming a guitar. "I mean, technically, he's the only one who knows."

LOW TIDE, 6:19 P.M.

I walk my bike home, my bag like a big old hunch on my back. I guide the handlebars forward.

I try not to look back at them, but I can't help it. Jeremiah fidgets on the porch swing. His dad folds his hands at the tall, wiry knees of his lap. They don't look like they're saying much. Maybe they're just taking one another in, letting the empty space between them jam up and fill for the first time.

I hear the ocean do the same. It pushes out from where it rests at the horizon and rushes up to the shore. My insides jitter with the memory of all the salt water I've swallowed.

The ocean knows what I can't.

Whatever I'm dreaming is important to who I am and why I'm here. And, like Ted wondered, now I know what

I *want* these dreams to be. I want them to be about a mother and a father. I want the people turning up in them to be a part of me, the same way Jeremiah's dad turned up here.

The tires of my bike spray sand, like pixie dust, as I cross over to our place, drop my bike to the grass, and climb up the tall porch stairs.

I step inside. Lindy's sitting with our ocean puzzle, and as the door slams behind me, she stamps out a cigarette, real fast. She raises both arms like she's surrendering, but I'm not in the mood for our game. I drop my backpack and slump on the couch next to her, twirling my fingers around a loose button on the cushion.

"What's up?" She leans over the jigsaw, studying it. We're working on a section of light hitting the water, all the dark colors bleeding into a silver gleam. Her hands run over the loose pieces, searching. I splay my legs out, lean my head back, and sigh.

"Jeremiah's dad's in town. He's the man on the board-walk."

Lindy's gaze shoots up. "That's Jeremiah's dad?"

I nod. "Mm-hmm."

"I thought he looked familiar."

"He looks just like Jeremiah." I twist the button around and around the loose string. "Do you ever think about my mother and father?" I ask. "Like, if they were to come back?"

Lindy shoos the thought away. "Don't worry about that."

"But what would happen?" I ask.

"We'd deal with it."

"I know I shouldn't, but I think about them. About who they are."

She doesn't take her eyes away from the puzzle.

"I always think about how . . . the parts of *me* might be in *them*."

"What do you mean?" she murmurs. I watch her fingers run over the pieces, the chipped polish on her nails, the big moonstone ring on her thumb.

"Like, maybe they love to swim. And collect things. Maybe they're curious, like me."

"You are pretty good at marveling at the world. You're a thinker." She goes back to the puzzle, flipping one small piece back and forth in her hand.

"I don't know. I guess I can only imagine who *they* are based on who *I* am. It feels backwards."

"Connections aren't made in just one direction." She moves the piece across the smooth table. Then she swallows, like she's pushing a worry down her throat. I know she doesn't like thinking about the past. Mine or hers. "What's this about?"

"I don't know. It's just . . ." I hesitate. "There were years before you," I say. "*Two* until you. Until the me I am now. Where did they go?"

She places the piece in the puzzle with a soft smack. "I don't know."

"Do you know somebody named Ti—" I'm about to ask when I see her fingers move toward something at her neck.

A necklace.

But it's not the moon snail necklace I made to match mine. It's all sparkly, with some kind of charm or pendant dangling from the end.

"What's that?" I point.

"Elder gave it to me."

"What's hanging from it?" I ask.

"An anchor."

"So, like . . . a deadweight?"

"*No.* Like where we met. At the Shaky. At the docks."

I shrug and reach for my own moon snail necklace.

She holds out her wrist. "Don't worry. I'm keeping mine here." The rope is tied around the leather cuff on her wrist. The shell dangles off like a charm.

But she always said she wore the moon snail necklace close to her heart.

I breathe in the stale memory of her cigarettes. The gold anchor hangs at the little pocket between her neck and chest. It fits like a perfectly kept secret, one I can ask a million questions about but never really get at, no matter how hard I try. I shake my head back and forth, fast. If I could shake off Elder and the necklace and Lindy's googly eyes, if I could shed it all like a stuffy winter coat, I would.

"Now, do I know somebody named *who*?" she asks.

I shake my head. "Never mind." Whatever's in me is *mine* to figure out.

I turn my attention to the countertop and gesture to the science-experiment bread on the counter. "Anything?"

"Nada."

"Too bad."

"I think it should be moist," she tells me. "Isn't that how mold grows?"

I shake my head. "I don't know."

"It lives where it's wet."

"You could have told me that sooner."

She laughs.

"So what do I do?"

I can see her trying to remember. "I think I put it in a little baggie. In the fridge. I feel like there was this whole comparing and contrasting thing going on. Between the dry countertop and the cold fridge."

"Yeah. That's a good idea." I stand up and move toward the refrigerator and open it. I package a new slice of bread, placing it in the back of the fridge. It's better than waiting for mold to grow where it can't.

I'm thinking about the stale bread when I hear Lindy say, "They don't disappear."

"What doesn't?"

"Those years. They're a part of you." She clutches her hand to her chest. "They're somewhere, inside."

I bring my hand up to feel for my own heart. Maybe I'm the wreck of a ship. The remains of a disaster at sea. Maybe I'm the stuff of fairy tales, a baby in a bundle left at the shore's doorstep, abandoned, so two parents can live a better life without me. It's hard to imagine it could be one or the other, so black-and-white.

There's more to every story. There must be more to mine.

As I thwack the stale slice of bread against the counter, listening for the dull thud, seeing nothing fuzzy or funked or even close to being mold, I know I'll have to find a way to get closer to the truth of these stories. There's a link, I'm certain, between what's there when I close my eyes to dream at night and what's real.

It lives where it's wet.

"I'll be right back," I tell Lindy before I grab an empty glass jar and slip open the screen door. The afternoon sun slashes in a wiry glint across the porch. I wind around toward the back, take the steps over the dune, and rush to the ocean.

I see the waves slide up the shore and back. Over and over. It's a tease. A game. But each time the ocean retreats, it leaves a little something behind.

It's like those scientists uncovering secret after secret of the *Titanic*. Clue after clue. I wonder what kind of clue

I might be. After all, I was washed up here, too. Then I wonder what secrets the ocean's still holding on to.

The glass is cool in my hands, and I twist off the top.

Swallowing it is capturing it. And if I can *steal* it, I can *know* it. My own way of tracking the wreckage of my past. I crouch to my knees, cup my hands around the glass, and wait for the tide to crawl in. Then I bring the glass low, letting the water bubble up and over my sandals and into the jar. It swells and sloshes over my feet, filling up the glass, and then the water slips away, snatching at the earth like a runaway crab.

All these years, I've been collecting the shells. The remains. What the ocean brought up to shore and left behind.

But now, I've trapped the source. A watery mix of sand and seaweed, yellowed and salty, swirling in its own murky glow. I bring the jar to my lips and take a sip.

HIGH TIDE, 12:21 A.M.

Adventure Park was slow in the rain. The swing carousel sat still. The seats of the Ferris wheel looked like a rainbow of buckets, rocking at the very top.

But the arcade was packed. Tink waited her turn at the Skee-Ball machines, listening as the ball clamored up the ramp, then sank into the holes with a song of beeps. It was almost impossible to hear with the other games going off and kids shouting at the Half Court Hoops, but Tink was in tune, *Queen of Skee-Ball*, at least that's what Len and Kimmy called her. She sank the hundred slots like it was nothing, and prize tickets would spool out of the machine. She was careful to fold them into a neat, rectangular stack that she stuffed in her pocket to buy the rainbow bracelets from the prize stand.

She glanced at Alexis, who stood behind the glass case at the stand, looking lonely and bored. Tink was next in line, and the Skee-Ball machine at the farthest end was almost free. One curly-haired kid had only two balls left.

But she looked back at Alexis, who was steadily rocking her elbows at the counter. She looked like she was willing to talk to anybody. So Tink decided to leave her place.

She squeezed through the crowds, keeping her eye out for Len and Kimmy at the Whac-A-Mole, and made her way to the prize stand, just as Alexis swooped up, waving.

Tink waved back, inching closer, until she realized Alexis's gaze was somewhere behind Tink. Wasn't it always these days?

She turned around. *Coop.* Of course.

"Hey." Alexis half smiled at her, then her smile widened as Coop came forward. He clutched the sleeves of his hoodie with his fingers, stretching them over his palms as if he was cold. She brightened. "Hey! Come on back."

He was obedient, slipped himself inside the little door that Alexis shuffled open, but she didn't let Tink in. Tink stayed outside the stand, trying to figure out why she bothered to even make her way over.

Alexis turned her back to Tink, stuck her chest out toward Coop, and dipped her head to one side, like she was in flirt mode. "So, a bunch of us are going to Tawny's after I get off. You in?"

"Sure. So, what's going on here?" he asked, and Tink watched as he ran his fingers up and down Alexis's arm, tracing it, over and over again. She felt somewhat sick.

"The usual. Bunch of nerd kids trying to get enough prizes to win junk like this." She took her other arm and ran it dizzyingly across the prize wall.

Tink could feel the wad of tickets stuck in the back pocket of her shorts and felt dopey. While Coop was running his fingers up and down her sister's arm, she was worried about collecting a bunch of cheap, plastic bracelets to send up her own.

She swung around from the counter and looked for Kimmy and Len in the chaos. They were no longer at the Whac-A-Mole. She shouldn't have strayed so far from the Skee-Ball machines. They probably had no idea where she was.

Alexis giggled behind her, and when Tink turned around, Coop's lips were at her ear just as Alexis pulled away. She caught Tink's eye, and her smile turned shy, not quite sorry, just sort of weirdly proud and ashamed at the same time.

"I'll see you later," Tink told Alexis, trying to leave the awkward moment as soon as possible.

"Tell Mom I'll be at Tawny's tonight," she called out.

Tink could barely murmur a "Sure thing" before rushing her gaze across the entire room, looking for Len and

Kimmy, anywhere. She reached into her back pocket and clutched the tickets in her hand. It was enough to get a few more bracelets, but she'd probably look dumb, anyway. What had Kimmy said it looked like? Like she had a Slinky toy strapped to her arm?

She let the tickets fall to the floor. Some lucky kid would swoop them up and get a bunch of *junk* from her sister, who was currently being nibbled and picked over like she was on the menu at a buffet feast.

She walked to the exit and out into the rain. She let the rain prickle her bare shoulders. It felt warm and comforting, in this weird way, like the rain was a cloak she could slip on and become invisible beneath.

The park was small. Just the mini-golf course, a Ferris wheel, and the swings. She walked to the wheel and fingered the bracelets on her arm. How many more did she need to make it to her elbow? She whipped her head back and forth, a reminder of *no, no*, what did it matter? *Cheap junk*, like Alexis had said.

She looked back to the arcade entrance. Coop stood beneath the awning and smacked the bottom of a pack of cigarettes against his thigh. When he lit one, he gazed out, and she thought she saw him nod at her.

She shook her head of rain and wandered toward the awning.

Coop took a long drag of his cigarette, closed his eyes, and let out the smoke. She thought of Len, fumbling with cigarettes at the marsh. What would it matter if she tried, too?

"Can I have a cigarette?" she asked.

He reached into his tight jeans and offered the pack. She swallowed hard, pulled out the long white cigarette from the crumpled box. She slipped it between her fingers, pretending like she knew exactly what she was doing.

"Need a light?" Coop asked.

She nodded.

He flicked the lighter, that *click-click-click* sound, and tried to light her cigarette, but she wasn't sure what to do. So he traded cigarettes with her. "Like this." He puffed her cigarette at the same time as the *click-click-click*. Then he offered it back.

She brought the cigarette to her lips, trying not to feel weird that his lips had touched it, too. She guessed that's how it worked. She breathed in the smoke, let it fill her lungs, warm and sweet and terrible. She wondered how Alexis kissed his smoky lips. She wondered if taking a cigarette from his smoky lips was like kissing them. She wondered why she was doing this at all. As if her lungs couldn't answer the question either, she felt a surge of saliva and smoke, but she couldn't cough, not in front of Coop, so she tried to swallow and instead let out a giant hacking bellow from her throat.

But Coop didn't seem to care or even notice. He flicked the ashes from his own cigarette to the ground.

"How's your canoe?" she asked.

He shrugged. "You're right. It needed a turtle."

"I thought so." She smiled.

"I can't wait for summer to be over. Every year, I think something is going to change. That it's going to be the summer of a lifetime, ya know?"

Tink nodded and coughed again, trying to catch her breath. She knew exactly. "It's never the summer of a lifetime," she managed to croak out.

"The promise of summer is way too much."

He sounded like a poet. She knew Alexis kept a notebook of poems she wrote. Alexis didn't write all bubbly with hearts over the *i*'s, the way she used to. She wrote in black pen and her handwriting was awful, and when Tink found it underneath her bed, she pored through soggy, sad poems about tears and rain and blackened hearts. Maybe this is what Alexis liked about Coop. Maybe they were their own kind of sad poem, together.

Tink brought the cigarette to her side.

"The fall. That's when things kind of find their place, ya know?" Coop asked, like he didn't care to hear the answer. "But just as it's lining up all nice, that's it. The year ends. And you think, 'Where did it go?' "

Tink whispered, repeated his words. "Where did it go?"

"Right?" he asked.

She was pretty sure she agreed. She was pretty sure

that the passage of time was probably worthless, every day exactly the same, and they would leave Barnes Bluff and go back to school, and she'd be rid of Kimmy, sure, but there'd just be every other girl, whispering and tittering over something she didn't understand, being ten steps behind when it came to noticing the *cute* kid, and it was all really *old* when it was supposed to be *new*, wasn't it?

"Right," she agreed.

She looked back into the arcade. She could see them, through the glass, in the dark, their backs leaning against the *Final Lap* racing game, Kimmy's lips against Len's, and he wasn't even pulling away. His hand was in her hair, like he knew exactly what he was doing, and Tink stood beside her sister's real-life poem, brought the cigarette to her lips, and breathed in.

She caught the smoke and swallowed it. She let it stay inside her, trapping it there as long as she could. She could feel it filling her. Then she let it out in one smooth breath.

LOW TIDE, 6:11 A.M.

My toes squish in the sand as the water bobs at my shoulders. I flipper my feet and lift my chin as high as it can go. When I reach for the sand again, it's gone. The water dizzies around me, and I swirl inside of it, trying to swim and stay in control. But the waves topple over my head. I take in long, choking gasps as the ocean drags me under.

I can't see a thing, but I feel the sea take me until I smash into the ground, my bare skin grinding against the harsh sand.

When I open my eyes, I feel like I'm clawing at the beach, but it's only my fingernails scratching the sheets of my bed. I'm awake now, and the sunlight from the window warms my cheeks. I take in a giant, full, roomy breath.

"Why're you dragging me here?" Jeremiah whines.

"For clues." I pedal my bike faster, then lift up on my feet, so I'm standing and soaring through the warm air. The boardwalk hammers beneath our tires, and we ride toward the end of the island.

"How far is it?" he asks.

"Just before the lighthouse."

Jeremiah groans.

"We're almost there." I point my chin toward the lighthouse. We've gone this far across the island before. But usually we stop and laze around for the rest of the day on the beach, eating sandwiches at Rocky's truck stop. This time, I just want to get to where we're going. "Come on." I speed up again, glad we went early so I can ride easy, with just a few dollars in the back pocket of my shorts.

"What're you expecting to see?" asks Jeremiah. "I told you. It's gone."

"I don't know." I stand up on my pedals again and point my arm out. "Look."

The old Adventure Park sign still stands tall against the milky sky. Its lights are burnt out, but the frame of each letter is still there, with a gem-studded capital A, and *Park* in faded, fancy script.

Adventure Park's a relic. There was an electrical fire that spread and smoldered, and sent the Ferris wheel up in flames. But I figure there has to be a small something left to see.

As we edge closer, though, it's not looking promising. There's a rusted chain-link fence and an empty lot. The pavement is all cracked, so grass grows up in between the pockets. The abandoned building of the arcade looks like nothing special, with the rest of the lights and signs and rides all torn down.

Jeremiah squints across the lot, raises his hand to shield his eyes from the sun. He takes a big sigh.

"I'm sorry. I thought there'd be more," I say.

"Well, we'd better turn around." He does a 360 on his bike, grabbing his handlebars and popping a wheelie up in the air.

I shake my head. "We've at least got to go in."

"In?" Jeremiah points to the wraparound fence. "How're we supposed to do that?"

But I'm already clamoring my bike down the steps of the boardwalk, resting it against the fence. I secure my foot through a loop in the chain, then shake the fence a little. It seems sturdy enough, like it can hold me, and I let myself wobble against it before turning one leg over and jumping right down into the sandy lot.

Jeremiah's whining from the steps. "Come on, Summer. There's nothing here. Let's go to Rocky's or something."

"You are *no* fun, Jeremiah Cooper," I call out, hands on my hips while I watch the stick-skinny kid wrangle his bike down the stairs.

"I'm just supposed to leave my bike here?" he complains.

"You're not *supposed* to do anything," I holler back. "Do what you want." Then I turn around and start walking toward the abandoned arcade.

I hear Jeremiah huffing behind me before long, skidding his feet against the pavement, kicking rocks, mumbling about *getting in trouble* and whatever else his little brain is warning him, but I'm not worried about anyone finding us. Lindy says sometimes it's better to do something and apologize for it later than ask permission up front. And who's around to ask permission from, anyway?

I stand at the entrance where Coop and Tink stood with their cigarettes. The arcade is tall and black and window-paned, with the light-up sign drooping from a bunch of

111

loose wires. I peek through the doors but I can't see anything with the glare of the sun and the dark tint of the window. I tug on them, expecting them to be sealed tight.

Instead, they open right up, and the musty odor hits me, smelling like sawdust and mold.

I try to hear the sound of the games, the roll of the Skee-Ball along the ramp, the music, and beeps. I want to smell the crust of old frozen pizza. But the place is mostly empty. Outlets and wires line the floors. There are tools and construction tape on the sticky floor. It's a big, black box of an empty room.

Jeremiah's voice echoes. "Told you there wasn't anything to see." The door shuts behind him. We're left in the pitch black.

"Prop the door," I scold him, and he mumbles again about *getting caught* and *what're we doing here, anyway?*

I take another long look around. I guess Jeremiah was right about there being nothing left. I guess my dream stays a dream, full of a hazy past I can't figure out.

I shrug. "At least I know it was here, once."

"So we can head back?"

I nod. "Guess so."

Jeremiah's foot holds on to the door, and I move back toward it. I look down at my feet. There's a small clump of paper on the black rubber floor. I swoop down and grab it, a quick smile at my lips, knowing exactly what it is.

"Whatcha got?" Jeremiah asks.

I hold my palm out. "Prize tickets."

"Cool."

We walk out into the sunlight, and it hurts my eyes for a brief second. I clutch the tickets in my hand, knowing they're probably not Tink's. They could be a million different kids', or some old tickets already collected at the end of a night. But it's like the painted boat. Something real.

"Come on," I urge Jeremiah forward.

"You want to go to Rocky's?" he asks.

We make our way back to our bikes, up the boardwalk, ready to turn around home with nothing much to show for our trip.

I shake my head. "Nah."

"What's wrong?" he asks.

The tickets sit in my hand, scratching up my palm. Too bad there's no prize, no reward, nothing I can claim. "I'm not getting any answers."

Jeremiah clicks the brake on his handlebars. "We need a new source."

I think of the ocean sitting in my stomach. "More water?" I stretch my hand out to the shore.

"No. The only other person we've never been able to ask." He grins. "Turtle Lady."

HIGH TIDE, 1:02 P.M.

"We're really going to do this, huh?" I ask as we stand in front of Turtle Lady's overgrown yard.

I hadn't been on the property since the first time Jeremiah and I trick-or-treated on our own. He dared me to try her house, even if the light wasn't on, even if we knew, or everyone knew, she was off-limits on Halloween.

I ran up to the door, rang the dead doorbell, then banged the metal knocker. She didn't answer, and I looked back to Jeremiah, who giggled from the sidewalk. Just as I was about to turn around, the light came on. Jeremiah fell silent, and I stood waiting, knowing she was behind the door and I was in front of it.

I never stayed to see what would happen. She was Turtle Lady and we were kids and I ran off, shrieking, as Jeremiah squealed.

On the Halloweens that followed, we carried our

pillowcases of candy over our shoulders, like sacks, shrugging when we passed her darkened house, not even bothering to try.

Now we are in front of it, and the car is in the driveway, which means she's here, she has to be. And there is no fence between us, no jar of pickles as bait, just me and my dreams and four arcade tickets stuffed in my pocket.

I take a deep breath, and together, we step over the weeds and up the hard stone stairs, which are cracked with mold and moss. There's the damp smell of dirt and leaves and wild branches from the birch trees hanging over the stairs. I push them away and march up to the door again, settling my hand against that cold metal knocker, waiting.

I listen and hear nothing. I try to see through the panes of glass at the top of the door, but there's only a glare. I peek between the branches to the windows on either side. The shades are low.

We wait, and Jeremiah sighs, taking his fist to the door and banging at it.

But there's nothing and no one. Not a sound. I'm not sure why I thought Turtle Lady would reveal herself here.

"It was worth a try," Jeremiah says.

I frown. "I guess."

"You got to go right away?" Jeremiah asks as we make our way back toward the sidewalk, where my bike rests on its kickstand. My legs are tired and heavy from the long ride to Adventure Park.

I shrug. "Why?"

"I wanna show you something."

"Haven't we done enough show-and-tell for the morning?" I feel the sting in my hammies, which is what our PE teacher Mrs. Godin calls the hamstring muscle in our legs. "How far is it?"

"Just at the landing." He gestures his chin toward the narrow canal between the ocean and the bay.

"All right. But then I've gotta get back."

He nods and we ride the yellow line away from our street, toward the next row of houses, where we can access the small boat launch. We hit the sandy edge and leave our bikes.

He doesn't have to point me toward it before I see it, something loaded up in massive clumps on the concrete slope of the boat launch, just past the slips. At first, it looks like dead fish in neat piles, but as we get closer, I see that it's a bunch of pink and purple lumps of starfish covering the entire slant. They don't move.

"How'd you find this?" I ask.

Jeremiah hesitates. He's got this long gaze that stretches out over the starfish and the ocean and into the dark. "My dad."

"He took you here?"

He nods. "Says they come in droves when the weather starts changing. They come with the tides."

"Are they . . . ya know?"

116

"Dead?"

I nod, and he shakes his head.

"I wondered the same thing. He says they're just waiting for the ocean to take them back. He calls them *sea stars*."

"*Sea stars*," I repeat.

"Poetic."

"I like that."

I look up into the sky, imagining those stars mirroring the ones that lie and wait here. The sun shines down on the starfish, giving them a wet pink sparkle.

"What else did he say?" I ask.

"He used to take my mom here. Before me."

"He lived here?"

He nods. "A year-rounder. Like us." Jeremiah nudges his foot gently against a starfish. "He's okay. I mean, like, not a bad dude. Not a jerk or anything."

"That's good."

"I think he's a little bit sorry. About leaving me behind."

"Of course he is." I like to imagine that my parents, whoever they are, would feel the same. Sorry. That they only got two years of me before I ended up here.

"I guess, with my mom dying . . . I don't know. He says he thought he was bad luck."

"Bad luck?" I ask.

Jeremiah shrugs and nods. "He says it followed him wherever he went. He even knew a girl who drowned."

"*Drowned?*"

117

"Yup."

"Whoa."

"Right? He didn't want it touching me. The bad luck, I mean."

"So, why's he back now?" I ask.

"I don't know, a few days ago he had some premonition or whatever. This feeling that something bad was going to happen if he *didn't* come."

"Deep," I say.

"Deep. I mean, it's cool that he admitted all that, right?"

"It is." There's this whole entire past that's a part of him. And he gets to know it.

I follow his foot with mine and gently rest it against a neighboring starfish, which curls an arm and hugs itself. My eyes dizzy over them all, so many, in these piles, just lounging there, wondering, waiting, trusting.

I don't know how they stand it. I don't know how they keep their faith, believing that the ocean will come and breathe its life back into them. Even if I know these tides as I know myself. Even if I know that they will come and go as sure as night and day. I feel furious for them. It shouldn't be like that.

Something shivers through me.

"They need our help," I say.

I reach down and grab a starfish. I do it fast. Before I can really feel its rough, sandpapery arms. I release my fingers and toss it back in the water.

Then I reach down and scoop up as many as I can.

Tossing.

Releasing.

It feels a little like I'm throwing pickles at Turtle Lady's window, like I'm taking something into my own hands that has never truly been mine.

I don't need to say anything more before Jeremiah follows. They don't belong here, the weather changing around them, pushing them, in clumps, up into this space, where boats slide into the water, where bare feet tiptoe around, where streetlights hover, instead of the moon or sun they're used to. They're stars, *sea* stars, and they shouldn't have to wait around to get to where they should be.

I scoop them, fling them, frantic, and I don't know where they land. I don't know if it's okay. I don't know if the ocean is ready for them. But they're ready. Of course they are. They belong in the water. In the sand. Not on concrete. Not here.

"Hey!" someone calls from out behind, and I don't turn around. I don't care.

"Hey!" The voice gets closer. "What do you think you're doing?" The voice is at my shoulder at the same time a hand is at my elbow, turning me, sharp and quick. It's nobody I recognize, and as Jeremiah swings around, I don't see any recognition in his eyes, either.

I look over at a beard-scratched face. Fishhooks dangle

from his rubber overalls, and knowing that's how Jeremiah rolls, it softens me to him. He's just a fisherman, out a little late, maybe, but we're used to them in Barnes Bluff.

I explain myself before I need to. "They need a little help."

"Leave 'em alone." His voice is gentler now. "The tide'll come for them."

I shake my head, about to explain, but he takes my elbow again. His hands are rough and worn, but his touch is light.

"That's the way of things," he says. "Don't intrude." He's stern about it, and I can see it matters to him. *The way of things.*

"They don't belong here," I argue.

He reaches down and handles a starfish carefully in his palm, like he's holding a flat leaf. Then he places it in my hand. "Feel it."

I feel the weight in my hand. It's bumpy on my skin but still and limp. I would swear it was dead if I hadn't seen that one starfish curl up onto itself.

"It's fine," the fisherman tells me. "It has no heart. No blood. No brains. Its blood is filtered seawater."

"Seawater?" I ask.

"It burrows. It waits. It shines. It holds on to where it came from. That's how it survives." His light eyes twinkle from his tanned, wrinkled skin. "It always belongs."

LOW TIDE, 7:16 P.M.

That night, I sit in bed, next to the breeze of the curtains. I clutch the jar of ocean water to my chest. I think of the arcade and Jeremiah's dad and Turtle Lady hiding away. I think of the starfish, full of seawater, always a part of where they came from. I take a sip, knowing, when I fall asleep, the ocean will become a part of me, too.

HIGH TIDE, 1:12 A.M.

They call it a *supermoon*, when the moon is closest to the earth, and there was one that night, with light pouring into Tink and Kimmy's room, keeping both girls awake, wide-eyed, staring up at the ceiling from their lumpy floor mattresses.

Kimmy was wired, saying how strange her lips felt from her kiss with Len, *raw and kind of tingly*. Tink ran her tongue across her own lips, tasting the lingering hush of cigarette smoke, even though she'd brushed her teeth for what felt like a million times.

"I hope it's not weird now," Kimmy said. "Between the three of us, I mean."

"*Now?*" Tink groaned.

"What's that supposed to mean?"

Tink had been too quiet all summer. She was tired. "It's *been* weird," she argued. "Not just *now.*"

"My mom always says that three's a bad number for friendships. Someone always gets left out." Then she giggled. "But I mean, now, Len and I aren't just *friends*."

Tink rolled her eyes, even if no one could see her. "It was just a kiss."

"It wasn't," Kimmy insisted. "We made out for, like, twenty minutes, I think. I don't know. I didn't time it. I was just, *in it*."

Tink knew. It was twenty-six minutes. It was twenty-six minutes of her standing with Coop, watching the rain, saying nothing, letting the cigarette smolder to ash in her hands.

She couldn't imagine twenty-six minutes of kissing someone. *How did you even breathe? And your teeth— did they knock together?* It sounded suffocating. She didn't dare ask Kimmy. It would seem like she cared.

"You never wanted to kiss Len?" Kimmy asked.

"No way."

"Did you ever want to kiss anyone?"

"Not really," Tink said.

"Never?"

Tink remembered sitting in a circle in the schoolyard as Piper Larson insisted they share their crushes, one at a time. It was nothing but this terrible recipe for hurt feelings, just so Piper Larson and David Rudy could announce a dumb crush that was already obvious. It was that way with all the kids who paired off. Obvious. Meaning it required no formal announcement in a dumb circle. Then all the proud pairs were boyfriend and girlfriend for what felt like two solid minutes before there was this weird string of dramatic breakups that secretly made Tink smile.

She remembered how red her face was, how she looked around the circle, trying to find some kid who didn't make fun of how short or chicken-legged she was. She settled on Chris Chilton, whose claim to fame was flipping both his eyelids up, so the red showed, looking like a zombie while all the girls shouted their *ewwww*s. She remembered how no one reacted to her announcement, not even Chris, who later took a *pass*, which she wished she would have done. She remembered thirty kids picking at the brown, sticky grass, mumbling who they like-liked, and not one of them said her name.

"I dunno," Tink finally answered. "Maybe someday I'll like someone enough to kiss them. But I've got better things to do than choke on someone's saliva for twenty minutes at the arcade."

Kimmy was quiet after that, and Tink didn't even worry if it hurt her feelings, what with the way Kimmy had ruined their summer with this dumb crush consuming every moment of every day.

They used to sit at night and watch the glow-in-the-dark stars on the ceiling and talk about anything and everything but Len. Now it was all there was.

Tink curled up and hugged her pillow, missing the old teddy she left at home because the stuffing was spilling out, and she was afraid it'd fall apart for good.

Tink heard the slam of a car door. Coop's car, probably. Alexis would be coming home from Tawny's. She popped up, listening. For what, she didn't even know. All she heard was pattering across the wraparound deck, then the screen door shutting closed.

She pushed the covers away and left Kimmy behind, opening the squeaky door and creeping across the second-floor hallway, which was like a balcony overlooking the rest of the house. They had rented the same home every summer for years, and it never changed. She loved the fishing nets propped up against the wall, the framed fly-fishing feathers, and the yellowing periodic table unfolded like a map and tacked to the wall.

She knew that the woman who owned the house traveled to Costa Rica every summer. Books were her thing. She had a library with floor-to-ceiling bookshelves that spilled over into untidy stacks. That's where Alexis slept, in a creaking foldable cot that sat tucked between all the dusty hardcovers.

Tink loved the old, mildewed smell of books. Every year, she tried to convince Kimmy to stay in that room, but Kimmy only crinkled her nose and called it *creepy*.

She rounded the corner and appeared at the doorway

just as Alexis pushed the door closed. Instead of leaving, Tink took a deep breath and knocked, hoping that Alexis was in a good mood.

Alexis opened the door with one hand, ripping a sock off with the other, hopping around on one foot. "What are you doing up?"

Tink groaned. "Kimmy."

"Snoring?"

"Blabbing about Len."

"That's still going on?" Alexis laughed.

Tink nodded.

Alexis shook her head and settled on her two feet. She had this far-off smile, like she wasn't in the room but wherever she was earlier, at Tawny's, with Coop.

"Come on," Alexis demanded. Then she grabbed Tink's hand, and before Tink could even ask where they were going, they were battering down the stairs.

"Where you taking me?" Tink wondered.

Alexis shushed her, dragging her out the screen door and onto the porch.

The air was cool, and it felt like there were a million stars in the sky.

"We're going swimming," Alexis said, like it was nothing. Like it was natural to escape the house in the middle of the night and swim in the dark.

"I don't have my bathing suit," said Tink.

Alexis laughed. "Who needs a bathing suit?" Then

she took off, barefoot, down the porch steps toward the dunes.

Tink wanted to feel whatever it was Alexis felt. A pull toward something. Anything.

She took a deep breath and followed, holding steadily to the railing, slipping her bare feet into the cold sand. The breeze ran through the thin nightgown that Kimmy had teased her for wearing on the first day of their vacation. Kimmy had boasted some new black tank and shorts set with peering cat eyes. Tink looked down at her own ruffled nightgown and tried to shrug like she didn't care.

The supermoon and the stars gave off the only light. It guided her across the sand to where Alexis stood at the ocean.

The sand grew wetter and colder, and Tink wrapped her arms around her chest as she approached. "It's cold," she said, quiet.

"Don't worry. The water's warm."

Tink grabbed on to Alexis's outstretched hand.

Before she knew it, Tink was waist-deep, her night-gown floating up around her like an inner tube. Alexis dipped her long hair back into the water, arms out. "I love it here."

Tink wanted to feel that way, too, the way she used to feel in Barnes Bluff. But she didn't. "It's not the same." She hesitated. "Without you."

Alexis laughed. "I'm right here."

Tink shook her head. "It's not the same. I'm so far behind."

Tink expected Alexis to ignore her, dismiss her, like she was a sad little puppy dog begging for treats. Instead, she stood up. "Being twelve stinks."

Tink smirked and repeated it. "Twelve stinks."

Alexis laughed. "It does. But then you grow up and move on and you're free of it."

She dove forward into the water and took off.

Tink lowered herself into the water. She moved in the slippery, cool breath of ocean to where Alexis popped her head up. They both floated on their backs together, looking up into the star-soaked sky.

"Are you in love with Coop?" Tink asked.

"In *love*?" Alexis paused. "Maybe. I don't know."

"It's possible? Not to know?" she asked.

"Of course."

Tink wondered if she would know, when the time came. Or if she would have to sit in a circle and announce it, the way she had to with Chris Chilton. *Chris Chilton*. Why, of all names, did she pick that one? "Does Coop write you poetry?" Tink asked.

Alexis shook her head. "He writes his own. It's not for *me*."

"Is it any good?"

"Sure." Tink could hear the shrug in Alexis's voice. "He said you two chatted at the park."

"I wouldn't call it a chat, really."

Alexis laughed softly. "What did you think of him?"

"He's . . ." She searched for the right word. "Soulful."

"*Soulful*," Alexis repeated. "I like that. You both are."

Tink couldn't help it. She liked being connected to Coop in some way. *Soulful.* Was she? She wasn't even sure she knew exactly what it meant. She imagined it was always being deep in thought. And she was. So deep, sometimes, she didn't know how to get out.

She felt the ocean beneath her. She felt weightless above it. She tried to quiet her thoughts and shed the jumble of feelings inside her. She tried being free of herself, for just a little bit.

"It's okay." Alexis broke the silence.

"What is?"

"It's okay that things aren't the same. That you're behind. It's a good thing. You're just catching up on your own time."

Catching up.

"Someday you'll catch up to everyone. To me. And you'll go so far beyond us. Just wait. You'll see." She flipped over and dove into the water again.

Tink stayed put, her fingers resting like feathers against the soft, rocking water.

LOW TIDE, 7:05 A.M.

I am folded inside the same darkness as Tink. But the cool water doesn't rest below me. I rest inside of it. My arms and legs spread out in the darkest, deepest part of the ocean.

I try to move. I try to breathe.

I can't.

I'm still and cold and alone.

Then I wake up. The breeze from the window slips across my bedroom, and I open my eyes.

After school, I pedal fast, then rise from my bike seat and soar. It's drizzling on and off, but I like riding in the rain. I like sifting through it, proving nothing can stop me. I do my best thinking in an end-of-summer rain.

And I've got a lot of thinking to do.

Because I can't decide if the dreams are like Tanvi said: just my dream world and my real world colliding in twists of mind and memory. Or a real-life thing that happened once. Dreams are messy, strange. I fall into them, headfirst, each night, but then they're the ones that end up passing through me. I can't decide if they stop when I open my eyes or if they live on, outside of where I am.

I can't decide what's possible.

I remember Tink again, weightless, resting against the water's easy flow. I remember myself, trapped in the deepest part of the ocean. I felt the water like it was my own memory.

But, then, maybe it was.

First, I pedal in circles, then I soar in one straight, steady line, to the marsh, to the canoe, to the place of my dreams, and I hear the sweet sucking sound of my shoes in the muck.

The skies darken, the trees toss their leaves, and with my breath heaving, my hair matted to my neck, I look out at a woman with a dress hoisted to her waist, rubber boots disappearing into dark pools of water.

Turtle Lady.

She eyes me with a shake of her head. "Can't leave well enough alone, huh?"

I find my voice. "Who is she?"

Turtle Lady sighs.

I stay where I am. Up close, Turtle Lady is wrinkly and doughy, and her breath is all wheezy.

"Nosing around again. You and that boy, what's his name?"

"Jeremiah," I whisper.

"Throwing pickles at my window." She grunts, and her hands go to her hips. Her dress falls to the water and sets it rippling.

"You hosed me," I say.

"Sure did." She laughs, and her dull eyes dance a little.

"Who is she?" I ask again.

"Who's who?"

"Tink."

"Tink?" She lifts her dress again and leans into the sand.

This time, I move closer. The water rises up to my ankles. It soaks the cuffs of my jeans, which nag tight at my calves.

It's weird to be near her. It's like being let in on a secret.

She points to the wet sand, and I lean over, staring into the pools of water and muck.

It's a nest of eggs.

"What are they?" I ask.

"Diamondback terrapins."

"Turtles."

"Mmm," she murmurs. Then she looks up at me and winks. "How I get my namesake around these parts."

"You *know*?" I ask.

She laughs low and long. "Indeed."

"What are they doing here?"

"What do you think they're doing here?"

"I dunno."

"Getting ready to hatch. It's September."

"What are *you* doing here?"

"We're not careful. We don't take care. Diamondbacks are on their way out. Spent my life studying terrapins. All around the world." She laughs. It's a small hiccup before she's stern again. "Turns out, the one thing I was look-ing for? Playing out right here in Barnes Bluff. In my own backyard. So I been keeping an eye. Before I go."

"Go?"

She grunts. "Answering the siren call, I guess."

I'm not sure what she means, but, then, not much of Turtle Lady makes sense.

"It's a small thing—terrapins," she continues. "A small thing in a big world. But. You keep your corner of it. Best you can."

"Four seven three," I remember out loud.

"She's keeping on." Turtle Lady rises up. "Against the odds."

I stare at the nest of eggs and ask what I've been won-dering all these years. "Why are you always hiding?"

"Hiding?" She seems taken aback.

"We never see you."

"I'm *here*, aren't I?"

"You're *here*, but you're not, like, anywhere else."

"People. They aren't my thing. Thought I'd made that clear." Then she takes a long look at me, her dark eyes scraping the surface of something. "So who's this, what's it . . . Tink?"

I take a deep breath. "I thought maybe you knew some-thing. About me. About how I ended up here in Barnes Bluff."

She laughs. "You thought *I'd* know? How you ended up

here? How does anyone end up anywhere?" she continues. "You end up where you end up. You make the best of it." She points to the eggs. "You find a way to survive."

My heart sinks. Just like everybody else, she doesn't know a thing.

The skies break open in rain.

Turtle Lady looks up, rain flattening her bun. "See. You got to worry about flooding." She looks down at the eggs.

"It's nice of you to care about them," I say. "But isn't that their mother's job?"

"Mmm," she grunts. "You'd think."

"It's not?"

She wades in the water and breathes all wheezy again. "Just not how it works. That's all."

I turn to go. My shoes rake over the gravelly sand and dirt and beach grass, then I climb over the gate to the side of the road, lift my bicycle handle, and sit with the rain battering my shoulders, soaking my hair, thinking of the terrapins, the unhatched eggs, Turtle Lady, after all this time, keeping up after them.

She doesn't know a thing about Tink. She doesn't know a thing about me.

No one does.

I soar off into the rain toward the Pitch & Putt.

I bang at the door while the rain beats down. The trees toss their branches in the wind. My hair sticks to the back of my soaked shirt.

Jeremiah slips open the door. "Whatcha doing?" he asks.

I poke my wet head in the hut. "It was locked." Then I shed my wet backpack to the worn rug of the game room. "Turtle Lady," I say, breathless. "She's keeping the terrapins alive."

"Terrapins?"

"Diamondback terrapins. Turtles. She's making sure they hatch. That's all it is. That's all."

My sneakers squeak toward the old couch, and I collapse into it, dust puffing out and catching the air, my hair tangled, my heart beating fast and hard.

"It's silly, isn't it?" I ask.

Jeremiah leans against the windows, fidgeting his fingers around his fishhooks.

"They're just dreams, aren't they? I just wanted them to have something to do with where and who I came from. But of course they don't. Why'd you let me think they did?"

He's quiet. The fishhooks ping against one another.

"It's silly," I answer for myself.

I catch my breath and let it fill me up as the rain beats down on the hut.

When I get back to our place, the last person I want to see is settled on our low couch. Elder. Lindy's next to him, all flushed and strange, like I caught her in the middle of something I shouldn't have.

Lindy stands up, real quick, with a dishrag slung over her shoulder. The air is humid and dense, and I don't know if I should sit or stand or run away.

I choose to stand. I stay frozen and rooted, feeling like my place on the hairy living room rug is the only place in our home that's mine.

"You're soaked," Lindy says.

"It's pouring."

"You should take the bus home when it pours."

I shrug. "I brought my bike. It's just water."

"Mmm."

Elder sinks further and further into the couch, making a permanent butt mark, all warm and sweaty. I feel like I'll never be able to sit on the couch again without his imprint.

I want to take the dusty shells and swipe them from the sills and hide them, along with the ocean puzzle, and the faded curtains, because everything suddenly feels too out in the open. I want to scoop it all up in one big armful. I want it to stay ours. Mine and Lindy's.

"I've got homework," I say, and I don't look at Elder, who I'm sure is staring at me, waiting for something I can't give him: approval. And why should I give it? He doesn't approve of me being around. He already made that clear at the Shaky. He wouldn't have done what Lindy did if *he* found me. He'd have left me there, like the terrapins, to fend for myself.

I sling my backpack over my shoulder and try not to imagine them watching me as I cross the rug and climb the stairs. With all the rain, my room is dark, but I don't turn on the lights. I sit, slumped on the bed, and I look at the space, at the buckets of shells, and my desk, stained with old markers from when I was a kid. The curtains are too pink and too lacy, and I don't know the last time either one of us washed them. The rug is linty and faded, and everything feels like it has a dusting of sand and salt, because that's what living on the ocean feels like all the time.

I should vacuum it like I'm supposed to. I'm seeing my room the way Elder would, instead of just being in it.

The bed is still unmade. I lean back on it, the backpack bulging behind me. I feel weighted down.

On my shelf sits a row of evidence that suddenly seems pointless, the lady crab shell, the crumple of prize tickets, and the jar of ocean. It's sandy and murky and heavy with memory. I rise up, wrap my fingers around it, and shake it. I've trapped it, but maybe I shouldn't have. Maybe I've taken the ocean from where it belongs. Maybe I've let it sit in the pit of me for too much time, salty and sick at my insides.

I think about dumping it down the shower drain, but, no, that wouldn't be right. I trudge down the steps and try not to see Elder, still there on the couch, or Lindy, with the dishrag still on her shoulder, her legs curled up on her kitchen chair, deep in thought.

She perks up a little as I pass. "Where you going?"

I shake my head, not knowing how to explain, about the ocean and my dreams, and the way I've caught it, in jars and within me, to try to understand where I came from. How do I say *I'm returning it*? How do I let her know I'm taking it back to where I should have always been, instead of here?

I let the screen door smack behind me. The rain has slowed. There's just this pathetic drizzle, enough to be annoying but not enough to get me even more wet than I already am.

I cross the deck, then the stairs, then the dunes, the same way Tink and Alexis did. I leave footprints in the sand. I squat to the ground and unscrew the lid of the jar.

Then I empty it.

Lindy sneaks up behind me. I stare at her. We look nothing alike. Even the necklace she made to match mine is now a bracelet. Nothing *real* has ever connected us.

"You okay?" she asks.

I shrug. I sit back on the sand and place the jar in my lap.

She points to it. "What's that about?"

I shake my head. "I don't know . . . a failed experiment."

She sits cross-legged beside me, letting her hands sink into the sand.

"I love you," she tells me.

I don't know how to respond. A few days ago, I would have said it back. But, all of a sudden, three of the most reassuring words in the world make me feel sad. Instead, I ask, "Why?"

At first, she laughs. But, then, it's like she can see I'm serious. That I need an answer to this. And she softens. "Because I don't *have* to, Summer. Because I just *do*."

It doesn't feel like enough. It never does. "But *why*?"

I ask again. I feel like I've been asking it my entire life. "That day you found me, what made you do it?"

She says it, like she always says it, "I figured you were mine."

"But what does that *mean*?"

"It means I just knew. I just knew it was the right thing."

"Like you just know Elder is the right thing?" I ask.

She nods. "Exactly."

I let the jar sit in my lap, and I push my hands into the wet sand. The water inches closer to us. "What if he's not?" I barely whisper, but then I find my voice and speak up. "What if he's not the right thing?"

Lindy is quiet. Her face meets the open sky, like she's drinking in what's left of this crummy day.

I wish she'd fight me on this, but she doesn't. She only says, "I don't know. We'll see."

I shouldn't let myself, but I wonder if that's what it's like with *me*. If there's a time limit to what's always been the *right thing*. If, at some point, we'll reach a day when it isn't anymore.

It's not cold, but I shiver anyway as the water threatens to hit us, just a few more inches to our toes. I don't like being caught in a weird and worthless *we'll see*.

At lunch the next day, Jeremiah's got some kind of pre-tryout meeting for junior varsity track. The kid might laze around with his fishhooks, wandering and poking at things most of the time, but on the track he's cannon fire, whizzing around in his fluorescent shoes.

He keeps telling me to try out for the swim team this spring, but I hate the stink of chlorine and how it dries out my skin and clumps up my hair. Salt water's softer and colder, and in the ocean, I don't have to worry much about my stroke being a perfect straight line. I just let it take me. I like the surrender.

So, lunch is just me and Tanvi, which isn't much of a lunch when you consider that she's spending the whole time reading another romance. This one's called *The Lace of Desire*.

"What's lacy about desire?" I ask.

Tanvi plops the book on the stone table and sighs, like she's had to explain this a thousand times. "It's a patchwork, Summer. It's holey and intricate and there's just a whole lot to it. It's not some straightforward thing."

"It seems pretty straightforward to me. You just, like, *want it* or whatever."

She rolls her eyes. "It's not an *it*. It's a *someone*. And it's never that simple. I mean, sometimes you question whether it's right. Sometimes other people can totally object to you wanting somebody. Like in sitcoms. How someone's always getting married and someone else is always racing to the altar just in time to say they *object*. Which is totally cliché, by the way." She lifts the book up and continues reading.

I raise my eyebrows at what she calls *cliché*, considering she's sitting with a book where the cover's all designed with a gold locket open to a heart and a woman strewn out in a white gown next to some lace curtains.

Still, I imagine myself running breathless to object to Lindy and Elder getting married someday, and it feels pretty satisfying.

Ted Light slides onto the bench at our table, not bothering to ask this time, and I wait for Tanvi's obnoxious sigh, which comes right on cue.

Ted's got his ketchup packets at the ready, and he holds one over a plate of gray meat, drizzling it on like he's decorating a cake. His movements are in sync with a tune he's humming, some piano piece he's trying to master, no doubt.

"So, what's going on with your dreams?" Ted Light jumps right in, taking the entire hunk of meat and gnawing on it whole.

"I'm done with the dream stuff," I announce.

I'm surprised when Tanvi drops the book's spine to the table again with a clunk. "Already?"

I nod. "I think you were right. I think it was just my subconscious, or whatever, getting all mixed up. Nothing real about it."

Tanvi presses her cheek to her shoulder, like she's studying me. "I never said it wasn't real. I said it was an escape. Sometimes I think dreams are realer than anything going on day to day."

"How so?" I ask.

She shrugs. "They must mean something to you. Or your brain wouldn't dream it. That's what I think."

"It meant something to me . . . ," I start, but I don't know how to finish. *It meant something to me,* but *what? It meant something to me,* but there were more questions than answers. *It meant something to me . . .* "But it *shouldn't.*" I settle on that.

"It's like forbidden love," Tanvi concludes.

I roll my eyes.

"Yes. Don't deprive yourself, Summer." Ted goes to

144

pat my hand, like he's some kind of grandma, but I swoop it away with a laugh.

"Tink's story isn't mine," I say out loud, and it feels good to say it. "And neither is that." I point at Tanvi's book.

"So what? I mean, *really*. Tink's story is fun to dream. This book is run to read. Dreaming it is like living it." She lifts up her book of lacy desire, but I can't let the idea go.

"I mean, you could have a *real* romance," I say. "You could have . . ." I hesitate. "Ted."

Ted chokes on his meat at the same time Tanvi slams her book on the table. "What's that supposed to mean?"

"It means you could *read* it or you could *live* it." I turn to Ted with a dramatic sigh. I know I shouldn't say what I'm about to say. I know it's not my secret to tell. But how can she keep doing that? How can she hold on to all these silly love stories when she could have something real? "She likes you, Ted." He nods in a fit of coughing.

Tanvi's eyes grow large. "That's not true."

"But it is."

"It's not." Then she turns to Ted, who holds up a finger, like he has something to say, his other hand to his chest. "Don't listen to her," she demands.

I fiddle with my own dull meat. "Your call."

Tanvi grabs her backpack in a huff. She swings it over her shoulder, grabs her book, and stomps off.

Ted catches his breath and asks, "Is it true?"

"Of course."

"Heh." He thinks this over. "Then dreams do come true. The aspiration kind, in this case. Not the falling asleep kind."

I nod in agreement, because last night, my dreams went blank. I already put them back in the ocean where they belong.

HIGH TIDE, 3:13 P.M.

After school, I ride up to the house and there's a pickup truck on the pebbled driveway. The front door of the house is wide open, propped up with a rock, like someone's coming and going. In and out.

The pit of me goes sour.

Elder.

And his *things.*

I groan when I step off the bike and let it fall. I peer into the pickup truck and wonder what he's bringing into our house. But it's just a bunch of fishing nets and empty buckets and some glass beakers on a rack. Probably equipment from his job at the hatchery. Seriously? Our house is going to turn into some kind of boathouse, isn't it? Stinking of ocean and fish and who knows what.

Elder appears at the door before I know it, his glasses

all cockeyed and his hair slicked back straight and a little greasy. He removes the rock and stands at the top of the porch, squinting, then waves down at me.

I don't wave back, but I don't look away. I stand rooted, feeling the pebbles beneath the heels of my shoes.

Before I know it, he's hand-hipped in front of me, squinting past the sun. "Scoping things out," he tells me before I can ask.

I wrap my hands around my chest. "It's just a house," I say. But that's a lie. It's *our* house. "It's pretty full," I tell him. "There's not a lot of room for your things."

He laughs. "Not to worry. I live light."

He *lives light*. Who talks like this? I shake my head. "And we have plenty of furniture already," I warn.

"You do," he says. "That's why I'm selling most of mine. Thought we could use the money for a trip."

"A trip?" I wonder out loud. "We don't go on vacation. That's why we live here." I spread my arms like wings, circling the driveway, the ocean, the sky.

"Well." He shrugs. "We could go somewhere else for a spell."

For *a spell*? I can't listen to him anymore. "Well. I've got somewhere to be." But I don't move. "Don't you?" It feels a little like a dare, but he's not taking the bait.

"Right-o. I have a shift at work. Getting the Hatch House ready for November trout. You should stop by sometime. They'll hatch in December."

"What makes you think I care about trout?" I ask.

"They're interesting," he tells me. "Genetically, they're more complex than humans."

"So?"

"It's worth knowing," he says. "That's all."

I stare him down, crossing my arms and not budging an inch. He shrugs with a small laugh and gets in the truck. He rolls down the window, taps his hand at the side of the car, and smiles all goofy. "I'll see you later, roomie."

I lift my bike and pedal as fast as I can to Jeremiah's. I go in through the Pitch & Putt hut, banging on the kitchen door, where I see him guzzling Gatorade at the fridge, wearing these flimsy little shorts that show off his stick-thin legs. The armpits on his white tee are all stained and sweaty. He's nodding at somebody, looking vaguely annoyed. I assume it's Gramzy, but then I see it's his dad, who is sitting at the kitchen counter, looking like he's lecturing him. I'm about to turn away when Jeremiah pushes the door open, fast. "Summer, you're here." He eyes me like he's been expecting me, like this is the story he's given his dad, and I get the hint that I better play along.

"You ready?" I ask.

He nods real fast. "Yup." Then he slams the refrigerator shut and waves to his dad. "See you later."

"What was that about?" I ask as he marches us both

through the hut, shaking his head, getting to the backyard as quick as possible.

"He's lecturing me about *you*. Saying he's got a bad feeling."

"About *me*?" I remember him creeping around the boardwalk, the first time we saw him, before we knew who he was to this place.

"Saying I should stay away from *girls*. I mean, you're not a *girl*."

"Um . . ."

"You know what I mean. You're . . . *you*. You're *Summer*. Besides, after twelve years, he can just waltz in here and have an opinion? What does he know? I just . . . I wish . . ." He says it quietly, like he's ashamed. "I want him to leave. He needs to leave."

He sits on the Pitch & Putt grass, and I plop down beside him. "Well, I'm not going anywhere," I say.

"Nope," he agrees. "He better get that straight."

"Besides, I've got my own intruder," I confess.

"Who?"

"Elder. He's moving in tomorrow. We should ship them away together," I start.

He snorts. "Toss 'em out to sea on nothing but a wooden raft."

"With prune juice and bologna sandwiches."

"Feed Elder's dog laxatives and send it with them."

Our laughter starts small, but it gets bigger. Until we're rolling with it in the itchy grass. Until it rages at the pit of my stomach and stays there. Until it hurts too much.

"I miss when it was just me and Lindy," I tell him.

"Well. There's no going back." He lifts himself up and shakes off some pieces of grass. "Come on."

"Where?" I ask.

"Wherever."

We walk across the Pitch & Putt toward the dunes. We skid down them, our sandals leaving a trail in the slope of the sand. We crunch over washed-up seaweed and I eye the shells. They stick up from the wet sand in pearly white and pink. There's the black of crusted mussels and smoothed-over beach glass. I think about snagging a few. I could put them in my pocket.

But I think of all the shells we have in the house already. They don't seem as special anymore. They all look exactly the same.

Jeremiah skips a flat rock across the water. It gets three skips across the surf and disappears. "I ran the one hundred in 11.57 seconds," he tells me.

"Is that good?" I wonder.

"It's real good. It's a personal best."

"How do you do it so fast?"

He shrugs. "I just tell myself to push a little bit harder. That's all."

"What happens when you can't push it anymore?"

"I guess that's it. I guess that's as fast as I'll ever go."

"Have you reached your limit?" I ask.

"No way."

I wonder how he can be so sure.

Soon enough, Elder's moving his things in for real. The pickup truck has more than just his fish gadgets. There are suitcases and boxes, sports equipment and a giant bag of dog kibble, which he lugs into the kitchen and plops on the floor. The dog's still at his old place. Apparently she had a conniption when she saw all their stuff shipping out, and Elder thought it best to let her calm down.

I don't think *calm down* is in her wheelhouse, and even Lindy looked skeptical when Elder explained. So I'm expecting we'll have this strung-out canine devil bouncing around the house for the rest of our lives.

It's sticky hot, and I stand at the porch, my elbows on the railing, not offering to help even a little.

"Iced tea?" Lindy holds out a tall sweating glass, but I shake my head.

She places it on the railing and nudges up next to me,

and we stare out at the boxes. "Elder's rummaging around in my room," she says.

I notice she calls it *her* room, but really, it'll be *theirs*. Maybe she's a little more nervous than I think. Maybe she didn't think this through. For a second I even wonder if she'll change her mind. Right then and there.

But, then, Elder slides out through the open door, slips a kiss past her cheek before bumbling down the steps for the next box, and her face turns that blushing pink again. I get that this is as real as anything. *Realer,* even.

I scan the front yard and look down the street. There's a giant truck at Turtle Lady's house. "What's going on over there?" I ask.

Lindy squints, shields her eyes from the sun, and shakes her head. "No idea." She doesn't look away, and I get this feeling she's just as intrigued as I am.

I yank at her wrist. "Come on. Let's see."

We walk down the steps, together, across the curved pathway, to the end of the driveway, where Lindy puts her hands to her hips and we both look out at the truck. There are two huge dumpsters, and men are coming in and out.

"She's leaving," Lindy concludes, now hugging her chest tight. "Or maybe already gone."

"She didn't tell me—" I stop. "I mean, I didn't hear anything about that."

Then Elder's next to us, wiping sweat from his brow. "Off to Florida, to live with her sister," he says.

We both turn toward him, quick, like, *How would you know?* And he answers without us having to ask. "Heard some people at the Hatch House talking about it. She is one of our biggest donors."

"No kidding," Lindy remarks.

"Got a thing for amphibians. Turtles, obviously."

Lindy's got this weird look in her eyes, still staring at the house. "Gone, huh? Just like that." She doesn't look away, and I see a gulp in her throat. And I get it. It does feel kind of strange, when someone barely anyone ever saw just up and leaves, for a place in Florida, for a sister we didn't even know she had, like there was this whole life she lived beyond us ever knowing.

"I'm going over there," I tell them.

"Leave her alone," Lindy says.

"I just want to see."

She sighs, but she doesn't argue. She's leaning back into Elder, and his arm is draped around her, like they're in some silly prom picture, and I take off before I have to see any more.

The closer I get, the more I'm confused about the dumpsters, which are as wide and long as garbage trucks and filled to the brim. Can someone have that much junk in the house? Is there that much she'd be willing to leave behind and throw away?

When I get to the dumpsters, though, the situation is stranger than I thought. I stand on my tippy toes and peer in. They're not full of furniture or household items. They're not packed with trash and crumpled-up old stuff.

They're full of books.

So many books, tripping and toppling over one another. Yellowed pages splayed open. Spines cracked and split. Paperbacks curled up like they've been read and loved and read again. Their musty smell is stronger than any ocean. It's a wonder the house could have held anything else.

I remember my dream. Alexis's cot pressed up against stacks full of books. They called her room *the library*.

I slip down to my heels and feel my breath quicken.

I look to the open door as some sweaty mover raises a lamp over his head and brings it to the moving truck.

I run toward the truck. The mover's head dips back; he's guzzling a bottle of water, Adam's apple pulsing in and out.

"Is she in there?" I ask.

He brings his chin down and looks puzzled. "Who?"

"*Turtle La*—" I stop myself. "The owner."

He shakes his head. "Naw. We were told to take everything but the books."

So the lamp goes with her.

The books don't.

"Can I take a look inside, just real quick?" I ask.

"Can't have no nobodies running around while we're on the move, kid. We're loading some heavy stuff in—"

I take off on the walkway before he can say any more. I

pass the old wooden door I've never seen open. The house is musty, and dust balls roll around like tumbleweed. The furniture's older and more antique-y than anything even Gramzy has in her living room.

I run to the center of the house. The stairs curl up to the second floor, and you can stand at the top and look over into the downstairs, just like I saw in my dream.

I scan the room. All the furniture's piled in the center. Against the walls are fishing nets. *Fishing nets.* I close my eyes.

The framed fly-fishing feathers.

I open my eyes and swirl around in a circle. There's a set of glass frames against the far wall. The feathers are pressed against the glass, like patterned butterflies, fluorescent and bright and hanging from hooks.

The yellowing periodic table.

I spin around to the space between the two windows where we threw our pickles. And, there it is, a giant periodic table, just like we've got in science class, tacked to the wall like an old map.

"I mean it, kid. We've got work going on." The mover sets himself up to lift a giant box.

"Just one more thing. I'll be quick, I swear." I don't wait for his approval; I just run up the old staircase, into the first room I see, and it's got floor-to-ceiling bookshelves, just like Alexis's room.

I stand at the door, my heartbeat slowing as I stare out,

through the window, at the ocean below. I can almost see them. Tink and Alexis. Racing toward the night, knees slicing above the waves, collapsing back into the water as they stare up, breathless, toward the sky.

This house is nothing like our house or like Gramzy's or like anyone's. It's Turtle Lady's.

And I've never been in it.

No one has.

But I dreamed it whole.

know who needs to see this, and I take her to Turtle Lady's just before dark, when I know the moving truck is gone and the house is empty and closed up.

Tanvi wobbles on her bike as we turn each corner. She hates any physical activity beyond holding a book to her nose, but I convinced her it was worth the trip.

"You shouldn't have told him," she scolds, gripping her handlebars like some old lady at the wheel of a car.

"You're right."

"It was insensitive."

"I know."

"I should get to tell someone I'm into them when *I'm* ready," she barks. "Not when *you're* trying to prove a point."

"So you would have told him?" I ask.

"No."

"I'm sorry. I just thought, with all the books you read, why wouldn't you want a love story of your own?"

"Do you know the statistical probability of a *middle school* relationship working out, Summer? It's like . . . abysmal."

"So it has to work out?" I ask.

"Isn't that the idea?"

I sigh. "What do I know?"

We reach the dumpsters, and I stand on my bicycle pedals, peering in. The books sit all lumped together, still and breathless. Tanvi maneuvers around on her seat, trying to balance, and when she reaches my height, her big brown eyes grow twice their size.

"She *threw them out?*" she marvels, shaking her head. Then she plops back onto her seat, gets off the bike, and puts the kickstand down. "Boost me," she demands.

"Boost you where?"

"I'm going in."

"*In?*" I ask. But of course she is, and I know there's no arguing it, so I get up off my bike and let it fall to the ground.

It's easy to lift Tanvi, who is pretty scrawny and latches on to the dumpster like a clawing cat. She props herself up and swings herself in, and there she is, floating on a pile of books with a big grin on her face.

I guess this is pretty much her happy place. Tanvi in her sea of books.

She rummages around, flipping them open, like she's just browsing at the library or the bookstore or something, and not sitting on a dusty pile of old mildewed books in a big plastic dumpster.

"Ugh. *Nonfiction.*" She scrunches her nose, eyes the front cover of each book, and tosses it behind her, digging for more. "You think the other dumpster is fiction?" she asks.

I think of the sweaty mover guy guzzling water earlier today and shake my head. "I doubt there was any kind of *sorting* going on, Tanvi."

"Hmm." She swings around, frustrated. "*God, Science, and the Galapagos. Reef Fish Identification. Avian Diversity in Ecuador.* Lame. Lame. And lamer."

"*A Guide to Long Island's Shores.*" She's about to toss that one behind when I stop her.

"Let me see that."

She drops it over the edge of the dumpster. I pick it up and brush off the slim book. The cover is a block of letters and endless sand, with a bit of ocean pooling in the right-hand corner. The pages are frayed and yellow, and the back cover lists the contents. *Shells. Brush. A Beachcomber's Guide.*

I clutch it to my side. "No romance, I guess?"

She shakes her head, disappointed. "What a waste." Still, she doesn't leave her nest of books. She crisscrosses her legs and settles in. "Maybe I'll have a house of books someday," she tells me. "Maybe I'll move to Florida with a long-lost sister. Maybe I'll do the opposite," she continues. "Instead of taking all my furniture and stuff, I'll just take the books."

"You could make a bed of them." I play along.

"And a desk."

"Keep them cold in the refrigerator," I laugh.

"They'll be in sweaty Florida, after all."

Tanvi leans back into her books, not seeming to care about dirt and dust and faded mildew. "It's strange. To not know anything about Turtle Lady after all these years. And to be left with this." She lifts her arms up into the air.

"I met her," I say. "I talked to her."

Tanvi's eyes grow wide. "You *talked* to Turtle Lady?"

I nod. "She's taking care of the diamondback terrapins. She's making sure they survive."

"So, she's not a people person. She's a turtle person."

I smile. "A Turtle Lady."

"I don't blame her. *People* . . ." Her voice fades away. "Are hard," she finishes.

She folds her arms behind her head and looks up into the sky.

"So, I think dreaming something is a little like living it," I confess to her.

"Told you." She grins, satisfied.

"But I also think you have to step out of your dreams

every once in a while. So you can figure out what you want from them."

Tanvi looks like she's thinking it over. "So, Ted Light really said that me liking him was a *dream come true*?"

"*His* words. I swear."

"He's ridiculous."

"He's nice," I say.

Her voice is quiet. "He is."

I grip the side of the dumpster. "I have an idea. You could wait," I offer.

"For what?"

"To be together. When the statistical probability of a relationship working out is better."

"True." She smiles. "It's best to set up for a happy ending."

With the night about to settle in, Tanvi and I part ways, her bicycle soaring off to the bay side of town and me wheeling up to the house. Elder's pickup truck sits in the driveway and it blocks Lindy's beat-up blue Civic, which means she's pretty much trapped until he goes somewhere. All of Elder and his stuff have landed where they're going to be.

I don't put my bike away. I let it fall to the lawn and look up to the house, with its rows of wraparound windows. The lights are on in every room but mine.

As soon as I step in, I've got a dog nipping at my feet, her bark all screechy and frantic, hopping like some bunny all over my toes. She scratches my bare legs with her puny little paws.

Elder comes rambling down the stairs. "Sit, Elsa, sit."

But Elsa boings like she's on an automatic trampoline,

and I try to wrangle myself around her. Lindy stands at the bottom of the steps, shaking her head and sighing. Her face doesn't look as bright and pink as it did when they told me the news of Elder moving in. I wonder if she's regretting the choice.

I look around the cramped first floor. There are some boxes of things. A bag of golf clubs sit with their own little tripod to prop them up on the frayed rug. A bunch of appliances line the kitchen table. There's a giant coffee maker and some red monstrosity with a spinning silver blade at the center. What little counter space we have is already crowded with weirdo empty Mason jars and lots of plastic Popsicle holders, which Elder sees me eyeing.

I can barely hear him over Elsa's yipping as he shouts, "I thought you might like Popsicles." His smile is too bright and eager.

"Oh." Why does he have to try so hard all the time? I make my way to the fridge to grab whatever Styrofoam box of leftovers Lindy brought back from the Shaky. Fried fish and soggy french fries, which I decide to eat in my room to avoid Elsa and the rest of Elder's things taking up space.

I don't bother to turn the light on. I let mine stay the only room in the dark. Elder rummages downstairs.

The fish is cold and rubbery as I eat it on my unmade bed. I pick at it with my fingers, and the grease lingers at my palms. I wipe them across my jean shorts and try to feel as sorry for myself as I can, eyeing the room and all the buckets, the shells, homework papers stacked on the desk, my schoolbag slumped on the chair, shelves toppling with the junk of being a kid, like a big hair clip clawing the hair of an old Barbie I haven't played with in ages.

I move the takeout container from my lap and make my way to the shelf, removing the Barbie, whose hair I expect to be all silky, like I remember it, but it snags through my fingers like stiff horse hair. I toss it in the garbage and it hits the tin can with a clunk.

Then I see the jar on my shelf. It's supposed to be empty, but instead, it's full of murky ocean. Before I can wonder how it got there, Lindy's behind me saying, "I thought you might need it."

"Huh?"

"The ocean. You emptied it the other day and I just thought . . . I don't know. With everything changing around here. I don't know," she repeats. "Something steady."

"Thanks." I do need it. I need it to get to the bottom of Tink's story. "Have you ever been in Turtle Lady's house?" I ask.

"A long time ago."

"Really?"

She nods. "A lifetime ago."

"Before me?" I ask.

She nods.

"Do you remember it?"

"Not really."

"Not even the books? She must have a billion," I exaggerate.

I thought she'd ask me a bunch more questions, the way she usually would, but she only stands at my shelf, running her fingers across an old music box. It's a ceramic pond with little magnet swans that float and swim when the music plays. "Why are you so interested in Miss Ellis all of a sudden?"

"I dreamed her house," I say. "I dreamed it before I could know it, and I was right. And I think there's something about me and the house and the people in it." I'm about to tell her all about Tink and Kimmy and Len, Alexis's cot in the library, and the painted boat near the bay, all of it, when Elder is at my door.

"Sorry to interrupt the party," he says, "but I'm looking for a screwdriver. A Phillips-head? I can't remember where I packed my toolbox, and I can't find one lying around the pickup," he rambles. "I checked the junk drawer, but no such luck."

"We've got a little toolbox somewhere." Lindy looks at me.

I shrug, even though I know the screwdriver is sitting in the hall closet with the cleaning stuff. It's in this monstrous, ancient-looking toolbox we never use because we just kind of let things fall apart around here unless the

167

situation's major. And then we just get Luss from the Shaky to fix it.

"Hmm. Maybe the garage?" Lindy asks, and she's already out the door and down the stairs, naming possibilities before I can finish what I was about to say.

I lift up the jar of ocean and turn it upside down. The sand and bits of seaweed and algae slide through it, like a marker of time.

I shut the door and let the room darken even more. I move without needing to see, closer to my pillow, and collapse on the bed with the jar in my lap. The Styrofoam container of leftovers squawks beneath my thighs, and I don't worry about wearing my sweaty shorts and tank top from a day at Turtle Lady's book dumpsters, the smell of fish fry, or the cold, sloppy meal settling into my stomach. I unscrew the lid of the jar, take a sip, and wait for sleep.

HIGH TIDE, 3:36 A.M.

"Then why'd you do it?" Tink asked, sitting in the sand, patting mounds of it into a bunch of domes. Not a castle or a pyramid or some fancy creation. Just humpbacks of sand for no other reason than she needed *something* to do with her hands.

"I don't know." Len paced, kicking sand at her knees as he shuffled by. "To see what it was like?"

She shook her head. "You shouldn't have done that. She likes you, Len. She thinks you're a *couple* now."

"I know. I know. I'm such an idiot."

"You are," she agreed. Anyone who would spend twenty-six minutes kissing a girl he didn't even like knowing full well she liked him was an idiot. "It also makes you kind of a jerk."

He stopped pacing, like he hadn't even considered the idea.

She rolled her eyes and dug deeper toward the wet, cool sand, grabbing another handful for her giant dome.

Len plopped down next to her, sitting cross-legged. His swim shorts were long enough to reach below his knees. He was so ghost pale he had to wear a T-shirt, and his neck and arms had a bright red farmer tan. "What should I do now?"

Tink stopped. She looked him over and shook her head. "You've got to be kidding me."

"What do you mean?"

She stomped off, moving from underneath the striped umbrella to the bright sun. Her one-piece bathing suit with bright pink watermelons was all bunched up with sand, and she didn't even care if she had a wedgie as she swung her arms and walked away.

The day was so hot, she could hardly stand it. The air felt dead above her, and barely anyone had stepped foot on the beach. She was counting down the days until they'd all leave and head home and she could be free of Len and Kimmy, at least, and have a week or so by herself before school started up again.

But Len had already caught up to her. "What's wrong?" he asked.

"You act like I want to be a part of the Len and Kimmy soap opera. You act like I *care*. Have I looked like I cared? This entire summer? Have I?"

"I don't know." Len shrugged. "It doesn't look like you care about much of anything this summer."

Tink groaned. She wished she were swimming in the dark with Alexis. She wished she were standing in silence with Coop, pretending she knew how to smoke. She wished that everyone would just leave her alone so she could figure out what she was even supposed to care about.

"It used to be the three of us," Len said, and it seemed like he had a lot more to say, but he didn't say any of it.

"It used to be the three of us," Tink repeated. "But then Kimmy went and got herself a crush. You went and got yourself an ego complex. And I . . ." She hesitated.

"*You* became all weirdo loner."

"*Weirdo loner?*"

He nodded. "Seemed like you wanted nothing to do with us."

"Well, isn't that *observant of you*." She stuck her chin up in the air and folded her arms.

"It hasn't been fun for me either, ya know."

Tink did not have enough eye roll left in her. "Spare me the sob story, Len. I'm sorry you had to *endure* the great love and total obsession of Kimmy all summer and then *suffer* through that epic make-out."

"I shouldn't have done it," he confessed.

"Understatement of the year." She stopped at the shore and dug her heels in the gooey sand.

"What'd we used to do around here, anyway?" he asked.

"I don't know. Eat hot dogs. Watch fireworks. Build sandcastles. Play at the arcade. A million things." But Tink knew it was more than that. It was going to the rusted old swings at the other end of the beach and seeing if your feet could reach the first branch of the nearby tree. It was getting so caught up in a game of manhunt, your heart would beat frantic in the dark. It was a water fight that lasted so long, you slept every night with a Super Soaker under your pillow.

Len seemed to know, too. "We used to have a lot of fun."

"I can't figure out what's changed," she said, but maybe that was a lie. She just didn't want to admit it.

"We did."

Tink and Len swung around, and there was Kimmy with her arms folded across her chest, speaking Tink's truth right when she didn't want to hear it. Kimmy was wearing a two-piece, and she didn't have a speck of sand anywhere but on her two bare feet. Her fluorescent-pink-painted toenails glowed up from the sand.

Tink wondered when Kimmy had marched up to them, how long she had been standing there, and what she might have heard.

"I feel like this summer's been great." Kimmy's smile

was so big, her teeth practically glowed in the sun. "It's Tink that's been weird, right, Len?"

Len sighed. "I don't know."

"I'm the *weirdo loner*," Tink announced. She kind of liked the sound of it.

Len smirked.

Kimmy's voice turned all sour. "But, I guess, it's Len who's been *suffering* and *enduring* this summer, huh?"

So, she must have heard it all. Tink expected Kimmy to march off, but she stood there, arms now at her hips, looking for an explanation.

"Don't look at *me*," Tink said.

Len stared at the ground, and Tink followed his gaze to the little grains of sand, to Kimmy's bright pink toes. He practically whispered, "I'm sorry."

Kimmy sighed, then she grabbed Tink's wrist. "Come on." She yanked her arm, but Tink shook her head. She didn't move.

"No," Tink said, firm. "I'm not a part of this. I never wanted to be a part of this. I think *you* two have a lot to talk about."

So it was Tink who walked away, leaving the two of them at the shore, staying the weirdo loner, which felt like the right person to be while she figured things out.

rock back and forth, caught in the shallow tides. My hair slips beneath the sun. Sand scratches my cheek.

Everything is still.

There's a small twitch at my fingers, then a hand nestles inside mine.

I open my eyes and stare up, expecting to see a wide stretch of sky. Instead, I look up at my bedroom ceiling. I'm awake and my hand is empty.

HIGH TIDE, 6:12 A.M.

I stand at the bottom of the steps smoothing my hair when I'd usually leave it wild. With Elder being here, I feel like I can't walk around in yesterday's crumpled clothes or have my hair sticking out all over the place from sleep. When I said he could stay here, I really didn't think it through. I'm in school clothes and my hair's all brushed, and I even scrubbed my face with soap. Twice.

But Lindy's like she always is, curled up in her seat at the kitchen table, her short hair in twisted bed-head spikes. She wears one of our T-shirts, a smiling clamshell talking on the telephone, with the speech bubble *Shell-o!* Coffee steams from her mug, and I know she's not quite awake until she's stared out the sliding doors to the deck for a while, until a few sips of coffee have kicked in, when she sleepily kisses me on the forehead and tells me to have a good day.

But Elder. He's something else. Eggs sizzling on the stove, the smell of bacon suffocating the whole house, his elbows knocking chairs as he twirls around the kitchen, humming along to some invisible tune in his head. He drums a beat with a spatula, which I want to grab from him and take to his face.

"Good morning, Summer," he practically sings as I make my way to the kitchen. And I feel like I'm walking some tightrope that's about to snap, with Lindy all sleepy and serene, like she always is, Elder buzzing around like some kind of frantic bee, and me just toeing the line in between.

"Bacon and eggs?" he asks, opening the oven and rattling around a tray of something with his gloved hand. "The trick is to put bacon on a baking sheet in the oven," he tells me. "Keeps it crispy. I saw it on *Barefoot Contessa*."

Even if I washed my face a few times, I feel like I'm half-asleep. I still can't figure out why he tells me things as if I care.

I manage words as best I can in all the commotion, making my way to the fridge. "I'll have what I always have," I say.

"Which is?" he wonders out loud.

"Toast," I say flat.

"Oh, I threw out the bread last night," he tells me. "Molded."

My eyes grow wide.

"There was also some stale bread on the counter. You've really got to keep on top of your perishables," he lectures.

I rush to the garbage. Even Lindy shakes her gaze toward the ocean and says, "Oh, Elder, no, that's—"

"Is it still in here?" I toss the lid of the garbage can open.

"Is what?"

"The bread." I stare at the bottom of the garbage bag. "The molded bread. The stale bread." But all I see are cracked eggs and the greasy plastic package from the bacon. The bag's empty otherwise.

"I threw it out last night. Today's garbage day. I printed out the garbage days on this handy dandy little calendar from the town website. Right here." He pats his hand on the fridge, where a sheet of paper dangles from a magnet I didn't even know we had.

I slam the lid to the garbage. "I *need* that bread."

"I told you, it's gone bad. I have English muffins, if you want that?"

I look, helpless, to Lindy.

"It was Summer's science experiment," she says. "On mold. She was comparing the moist, cold bread to—"

"The dry, stale bread," I finish for her. Then I take off, barefoot, out the screen door, down the front steps, and across the patchy lawn to the garbage cans.

But they're already on their sides, lids tossed, rolling around like empty barrels. The garbage truck already came.

I kick one of the barrels as hard as I can and watch it roll across the lawn. I don't even bother to pick any of them up and drag them underneath the porch where they belong. If Elder's so concerned about his precious garbage days, he can do it himself. Instead, I stomp up the stairs, slam the screen door, though I don't even know where I'm heading because I'm still hungry and there's the smell of bacon all over the house, and English muffins instead of toast, and I can't understand how we are where we are.

"I'm sorry, Summer," Elder says as I stand with my back to the door. I don't know if I should be coming or going. I feel as stuck as I did when Lindy made *me* decide whether or not to let him move into this house. "I had no idea. When's it due? How can I help?"

"You've been a big enough help already," I sulk. "It took weeks to get the mold going, and it's due this week and there's no way . . ." I let my voice trail away. What's the point in trying to explain?

Lindy picks up where I left off. "We could try something else?"

"*We?*" I wonder out loud. "What *we?*" I feel like I've been looking for our *we* ever since she asked Elder to move in.

"I could help. I mean, there's never any guarantee in an experiment, right?"

"No," I say. "There's not." I feel the heat rising from

my insides, burning up my cheeks, and I feel my voice getting louder. "It's like this dumb 'Elder moving in' experiment, which I can't believe I agreed to, because it has to be one of the dumbest ideas I've ever heard in my life. Second only to the dumb idea of you two being together in the first place."

Lindy's voice is soft. "Summer." She reaches out for my arm, but I pull away.

"You come in here, like you own the place," I shout at Elder. "But you don't. I thought *we* did." I point my finger between the two of us, me and Lindy. "But I guess it was always just *you*. I guess I've only been a guest all these years."

"You know that's not true," Lindy says, and her voice is so calm, I want to slap some sense into it. I want to send scalding-hot coffee across her lap and wake her up to everything she's ruined.

But I don't. I scoop up my schoolbag, push back on the door, and decide on *going* for good.

walk through the motions of school, spinning the dial on
my combination lock, slamming my locker closed, dragging my backpack from one class to the next, slipping into
one cold metal seat, rising up and settling into another.
I watch videos, scribble notes, swallow hard when Mrs.
Grady excitedly announces our science project is due at
the end of the week.

I try to stay numb to the morning. I think of Len and
Kimmy and Tink on the beach, instead. An image that
stays as the dream fades. The three of them in harsh sunlight. The uneasy feeling in my stomach as I move through
waking hours and they stay frozen in time.

After school, I sit on the bleachers along the track
with my homework and glance up every now and then to
watch Jeremiah race around it. The track is this blazing

burgundy color, and the kids look like a bunch of maggots swirling around a slab of meat.

"I don't want to go home today," I tell him as he finishes tryouts and plops himself next to me on the metal bleachers.

"Okay."

"Wanna camp out?" I ask.

"All right," Jeremiah agrees. And I'm glad for his easy way.

We bike to his place, and Gramzy eyes us both carefully when we tell her we're staying on the beach for the night. "Lindy knows where you're at?" she asks me.

I bob my chin up and down, real fast, too eager, I realize. "Of course."

She grunts a little, with a stern nod, and I know she'll be telling Lindy where I am.

It bugs me that I *do* care if Lindy worries. It bugs me *more* to know she won't have to as long as Gramzy tells her where I am.

But that's life in Barnes Bluff. Everybody knowing everybody's business. It's a wonder Turtle Lady managed to shut herself up inside a fortress of books. It's a wonder I have no clear past for anyone to even gossip about.

A small thought starts chewing at me: *Who else in Barnes Bluff has ever been able to appear and disappear?*

"You wanna do the tent or just sleeping bags near

the bunker?" Jeremiah asks as we fill my backpack with granola bars and a thermos of some fluorescent punch Gramzy's got in the fridge.

"The bunker," I choose. *The bunker* is what we call the three slats of old wooden fence that make a little shelter just past the dunes.

We walk through the hut and across the Pitch & Putt greens, then cross over the dunes to the bunker, steering clear of what looks like a big wet rock. But, when I catch the blob of paint marking it, my eyes grow large. I scoot down and watch as the rock steps forward and becomes what it's always been: the shell of a turtle.

I check for the tag at its leg. "Four seven three!" I shout.

Jeremiah rushes over and crouches beside me. "It totally is."

I look out at the Pitch & Putt over the dunes. "Made it all this way."

"Pretty epic."

We watch it creep forward.

"What do we do?" Jeremiah asks.

I think of Turtle Lady. "Just . . . let it be, I guess."

We watch it for a few moments, sneaking forward an inch at a time. It looks at us. Or past us. It's hard to tell. Turtles have this bored way of looking at the world.

I set the sleeping bag on the sand next to it and plop down on top of the itchy cotton.

Jeremiah lies down next to me, hands behind his head.

"Elder threw them *both* in the garbage?" he asks, like he just woke up from a sleepy conversation we had after practice.

"Mm-hmm."

"What are you going to do for the science project now?"

I shrug. "Maybe I'll be gone before that."

"So dramatic," Jeremiah says. "Gone? Where would you even go?"

"I don't know. I've never been farther from here than the lighthouse," I say.

"But that's as far as you can get on the island anyway."

"Right."

"You could head the other way," Jeremiah suggests.

"The city?"

He nods. "Sure."

"You think I could bike all the way there?" I ask.

"Course."

"But how would I even get there?"

"I mean, I don't know, you just keep going. Follow the ocean to the other end."

He's making some sense. I scrunch up my nose. "That's where Elder's from."

"What's he doing *here*, then?"

I sigh. "Trust me, I'm asking myself the same question."

The ocean creeps up toward us, then runs back to where it came from. There's a line that marks the tide from the morning. Brushwood sits in a neat row, just a few feet from the bunker. I imagine the tide reaching us tonight, just another way for the ocean to let me know it's left something of itself behind.

"How are things going with your dad?" I ask.

"It was all fine. I kind of didn't mind him after a few days. But he can't be telling me to quit hanging with you."

"He's still on that kick?" I ask.

He nods. "Gramzy's telling him to simmer down. She's trying to get him to concentrate on me running track. He's never even been to a meet."

"He's missing out."

"That's what happens when you abandon your kid, Summer." Then he swallows hard. "I mean, *you* know. Somebody's always missing out."

I nod, even if we're both looking up at the night sky. The sun has officially slipped away. "It's worse to not even know what you're missing out on."

"Or maybe it's better?" Jeremiah poses the question.

"I don't know." And that seems to be the only answer to everything these days.

I close my eyes and listen to Jeremiah unzipping his sleeping bag, a sign he's moving toward sleep. I settle into my own sleeping bag, my feet poking at its saggy bottom, because I'm outgrowing the kids' size. My head barely covers the cushion, with my hair spread out in the sand. Most people who don't like the beach don't like it because of the sand, how it gets in every nook and cranny of their bodies. But I've always loved it. It's how Lindy found me. She said I was sitting up in my bathing suit, building mounds of shapeless castles on the beach.

I yawn, listening to the tide's easy back-and-forth, my head sinking deeper into its cradle of sand.

LOW TIDE, 12:22 A.M.

Tink sat on the back porch, curled up in her nightgown on a rusted old patio chair. They had long finished dinner at the big, round table, where Kimmy did not try to squeeze herself right next to Len for the first time all summer. Tink had even managed to ignore any whispered conversation that Kimmy tried.

A leftover pile of unused napkins rolled up and over the rock that held them down from the wind. Everyone was getting ready to sleep. Tomorrow would be their last day in Barnes Bluff, and it was a tradition they'd take the early ferry to Shelter Island for the day.

But Tink had sneaked down while Kimmy was brushing her teeth, and she would stay there until she heard Alexis slam the car door again, after another night out with Coop, their *last night*, Alexis had sighed, while running mascara over her dark lashes and smacking her lipstick between her lips with a breathy *pop*. Some people looked trashy in red lipstick, but Alexis managed to look fierce and strong. Tink wondered if she could manage the look someday. Probably not.

She waited, wanting to re-create the night of that midnight dip in the ocean, with the nagging feeling that things like that couldn't actually happen every night, that the moment had come and gone already, but like a little kid, she hoped she could have it back once more.

She brought her knees up to her chest and looked out at the empty Pitch & Putt next door. It was getting cooler the closer they all edged toward September, but, like always, she'd leave before she ever knew this place in the cold.

The screen door opened, and Tink swung around in her seat. She saw the little black tank and short shorts, and heard the sparkling jelly sandals clack across the deck.

Of course it would be Kimmy. Of course she'd be cornered this late at night.

But it wasn't like she could avoid her forever. They'd be trapped on an actual *island,* even, the next day.

Kimmy wrapped her arms around her chest. "Was wondering where you went."

Tink shrugged. "Waiting up for Alexis."

"Is she out with Coop?"

Tink nodded.

"Must be nice to spend the summer with someone who actually likes you back." She groaned and squeezed into another mismatched patio chair.

Tink knew Kimmy expected her to respond, but she wasn't sure what Kimmy wanted her to say. So they sat in their pajamas. Kimmy squeezed her arms tighter across her chest. "I can't wait to go home."

Finally, something Tink could agree with. "Me too."

"Look. I know you expect me to apologize for stealing Len away this summer, but I'm not going to."

"I don't expect anything."

"Good." Kimmy's voice went quiet. "It's not like I don't know it should have been you two."

Tink placed her bare feet on the cold deck. "What?"

"You and Len. It's probably the better match."

"I don't want Len. I don't want anybody."

"Yeah. What's up with that?"

"Everybody's all . . . I don't know . . . *involved* with that kind of stuff," Tink complained. "I'm just *not*. And . . ." She hesitated. "I mean, maybe you should be less, ya know, involved. Maybe." She expected Kimmy to jump down her throat and disagree, but instead, Kimmy nodded and said, "Probably. I feel pretty silly about it."

"You should—" Tink wanted to say, but at the last minute, she added, *not*. "You shouldn't," she repeated. "Len should have been honest with you. That he didn't have feelings or whatever." She couldn't believe she was having this conversation.

"So you, like, knew?" Kimmy asked.

"Yeah. I knew."

"You should have told me."

Tink was about to protest, but then she softened. She told the truth. "I didn't want to upset you." She suddenly realized why Len might have acted the way he did. Even if it was cruel. Maybe *she* was cruel in her own way. Maybe they were all cruel to one another and that's just the way it was with them now.

"Do you think we'll come back here, like our parents do every year?" Kimmy asked. "All of us together with our own families and kids or whatever?"

Tink wondered. "I don't know."

"It would be nice. If we did, right?"

Tink could hardly imagine it, but she agreed anyway. "Sure."

Kimmy unwrapped her arms and stood up from her seat. "Come on. Let's find our *one thing*."

Tink knew what she meant. She smiled and stood up. They walked in the dark, holding on to the wiggly railing of the deck. They climbed down the steps and across the walking path over the dunes to the water. It was warmer than the air, and it felt like wet sun beneath her toes.

Kimmy bent to her knees and reached her arm into a little pool of water. She held up a large, slippery conch shell. In the dark, it shone white and pearly, and she held it up to Tink.

Tink reached out and ran her fingers across it. It was smooth and cold and strange.

They did it every year. They walked to the end of the point, a line of raised rock that stretched out into the ocean. They tiptoed beneath the moon and sat together at the edge.

Kimmy held out the shell and said what she always said, this strange prayer that just made sense to them.

"Let the stars see it," she whispered.

Then she handed the shell to Tink, who tossed it in the water.

Tink loved the ritual. The idea that the stars in the sky might be too far away to see her. That she might not always have to look to them. That, for one brief moment, they might look down and find her instead.

They sat in silence for a bit. The silence Tink had craved from Kimmy all summer. Maybe she would miss her, after all. Maybe next summer things would be different between them. No, not maybe. They *would* be different. She had figured that much out. It was just a matter of what *kind* of different. Maybe that would be the way things were with Kimmy from then on.

Kimmy yawned and stretched her arms up to the sky. "I'm tired," she announced. "You ready for bed?"

"I'm going to wait up for Alexis a little longer. But I'll head back with you." Tink dangled her legs from the rock and took one last look at the little path of moonlight reflected in the water. "It's a good spot, don't you think?"

"It's always been a good one."

They made their way back to the porch.

Kimmy paused at the sliding glass doors before heading inside, as Tink sank back into her wobbly patio chair. She expected Kimmy to say something sappy, like they were in some *I'm sorry* scene of an after-school special on television, but instead, she just said, "I'll see you in the morning."

"Shelter Island," Tink confirmed.

"It'll be fun."

As Kimmy slipped inside, Tink allowed herself to believe that it actually might be fun.

She leaned back in her chair and saw the lights of a car swing around in the pebbled driveway, flashing across the side of the house.

It was Coop's rattling old Jeep, which sputtered and stopped. The lights faded to black as the engine turned off.

The door slammed, and she waited for Alexis's pitter-patter across the deck, but instead, another door slammed and Tink heard the crunch of heels against the pebbles, two people walking toward the steps, and Tink felt herself shrink in the darkness. Even if she was a flight above them, hovering on the deck, she remembered the way Alexis and Coop had nestled against one another at the arcade.

She was about to go inside, not wanting to have to sit through some terrible kissing and slurping goodbye, but there was also something about the anticipation of it that made her insides flutter. The idea that it wasn't her, but it could be, someday, and it made her face turn flush in the dark of the night as she waited for the sound of them, embarrassed for them, for herself, for someone she wasn't yet.

When Alexis giggled, Tink stood up and made her way to the glass doors. As she opened them, their squeak seemed to stop whatever had been set into motion for all three of them. She heard their murmured conversation turn louder, and it was Coop's voice that said, "It's too dark."

"Come ooo-on." Alexis's voice was singsong, urging him, in her bored way, the way she had wanted Tink to set off the fireworks that night on the beach, like she couldn't care less, and somehow, that made Tink care more.

"You've been drinking," Tink heard Coop say, his voice flat.

Tink felt a little sick, thinking of Alexis drinking. She remembered Alexis sneaking jugs of their grandfather's wine from the downstairs refrigerator at their house when she was supposed to be babysitting Tink last school year.

Alexis's lips and teeth had been stained red, and she started laughing a little too hard as she continued tipping back the glass bottle. The label read CARLO ROSSI. *Cheap wine that old Italian men drink*, Alexis had said with a hiccup-y laugh.

Tink stood at the glass doors and listened as Alexis and Coop took off beneath the deck. She heard their feet thunk over the boarded path to the beach. She guessed they'd go swimming, the two of them. Not with Tink, of course, and she felt silly for thinking it might have ended up that way.

Alexis had said it was *their* last night. That meant her and Coop's. Alexis wouldn't want her little sister ruining it, with some floaty midnight swim to talk about Tink's dumb, little-kid problems in the Len and Kimmy soap opera.

From the height of the deck, Tink watched them run toward the water below. Alexis was a full sprint ahead, making some kind of whooping sound. Coop was behind, slower, even if his gargantuan legs were longer, and Tink could tell, by the way he stopped at the water, like a line had been drawn, that he wasn't excited at all by what was happening.

But Alexis plunged in, her knees crushing the waves as she pushed over the surf into the black of the ocean.

Tink stepped inside, about to close the door, not

knowing, never knowing, what made her turn around, except maybe the moon's light, disappearing. The chill of that as it slipped over her.

Before she knew it, she was across and down and over, her feet at the water. It was warm and freezing, both at the same time, and Coop was there, beside her, shouting Alexis's name. She could see the break in the tide. The way the waves crashed into one another. But she could not see Alexis.

rush the water, coursing through the force of each wave. I push against the ocean when it pulls me. I chase after it when it slips away. I have to get to where she is.

Alexis.

I know it's up to me.

"She can swim," Tink called out over the waves. She was farther than she'd ever gone in the ocean, and there was no touching the bottom. There was no sense of where she was, especially as she felt the rift in the tide, and she couldn't tell where Alexis had gone. Only that Coop was somewhere near, calling both of their names.

Still, she believed it all was okay, that everything would be okay. "She was born to swim," she whispered.

The whisper's at my heart, even as the water slips over my head, and I'm above it and below it, above it and below it, waves crashing over me in the dark, as I try to see what I cannot see, as I feel the water battering at my insides, memories rushing at my dreams.

If I could just get to her, wherever she is, if I could swim a little farther, then it would all be okay, everything would be okay, just like Tink knew.

I feel a hand at my wrist and swing my head around.

"Coop?"

"It's okay, Tink, I've got her," he says in between huge gulping breaths, and he turns to her, to the girl in my dreams, and I see her, for the first time. *Tink*.

I close my eyes and surrender.

HIGH TIDE, 6:51 A.M.

My chest heaves as I take big, long, painful breaths. I feel the wet sand at my back.

I open my eyes. Jeremiah's dad and Lindy sit over me on the shore.

"Where's Alexis?" I manage to ask, my throat scratchy and sore.

Lindy's eyes grow large. "Alexis?"

"She was there. She was—"

Lindy brings a finger to her lips. "Shhh. It's okay." Her other hand is in mine, so small and slender, it almost feels like I'm the one comforting her. "Let's get you up."

I have so many questions as I look from Jeremiah's dad to Lindy, as I feel the weight of Alexis, gone from my dreams, gone from here. I twist over to my side and see Jeremiah running toward me, wiping his eyes and nose like he's been crying.

"You were like a wild thing," he tells me in between snot and breaths. "You just took off, in the water, just swimming farther and farther, and then I got my dad. And Lindy, I don't know, Lindy was just . . ."

". . . here," I finish for him. Because, Lindy is always right here.

"I was dreaming," I tell him.

Lindy shushes me again and helps me stand. My legs are wobbly at first, but soon I'm up and the ground is sturdy beneath me as I find my balance.

I look between Lindy and Jeremiah's dad again. I feel them, in the ocean with me, in my dreams, all of us, trying to swim toward someone, toward *her*, and a wave of familiarity hits me so hard, I can barely find my breath.

Tink smoking cigarettes for the first time, Coop and his poems, a room full of books, a riptide so strong, it tore them apart and brought us all here. My breath quickens, my heart a metal knocker against my chest. The dreams were mine, but they were also theirs.

"You're Coop," I whisper at Jeremiah's dad.

He nods yes and his brow furrows, confused.

Then I take a long look at Lindy. "Tink."

"Thanks for outing me, Coop." She laughs. "I haven't been called that in a *very* long time."

"No, no." I shake my head. I don't know how to tell them that I've known them beyond this moment here and now. Then I realize the only way for them to understand.

"Alexis," I say. I'm about to ask it, but instead, I state it, because I just *know*. "We couldn't save her," I whisper. "She didn't make it."

Lindy swallows hard, shaking her head, trying to understand. "How could you possibly know about that?"

"I dreamed it," I say. "I dreamed you all." Then I tell them everything, like it's the biggest confession I've ever made in my life.

tell them about swallowing the ocean, about a story wrapping itself up inside my dreams, the firecrackers, Len and Kimmy, rainbow bracelets, and Skee-Ball. There's the painted canoe. Adventure Park. Kimmy and Tink's end-of-summer ritual. I tell them as much as I can remember from each dream. It spills from me.

I bring us all toward now, when we met in the ocean and crashed, like waves, into one another's lives.

"It was *your* summer," I tell Lindy and Coop. "I dreamed it."

Jeremiah is nodding away. "It *was* the before." His voice has this celebration whoop in it. He waves his arm to the ocean. "It's got a whole history. Like the remains of the *Titanic*. You can track it." Then he lifts his finger and twirls it around. "The swirl."

"The swirl." I smile.

Lindy's hand grips mine tight. I can see her processing everything I've said. "I'd almost forgotten about the painted canoe," she marvels. "And the dud firecracker."

"You and Coop, you talked outside Adventure Park. You shared a cigarette," I say.

She and Coop look between each other. "My first one. I remember that."

He laughs. "Me too."

She shakes her head. "How could you know this?"

"I swallowed your memories," I say. "The ocean let me dream them. I don't know how, but it did."

She shakes her head again. "I never told her," Lindy says to Coop. "I erased that day. I thought I erased everything. It's not possible for her to . . ." Her voice fades. "It's not possible to know." She grips my hand tighter. "But . . . you *know*."

I nod.

Jeremiah's dad has been listening, intent, letting it all sink in. "I felt like I had to come here, like something terrible was about to happen," he confesses. "I didn't want Jeremiah around you, Summer."

I remember what Jeremiah said. That bad feeling. My dreams and his premonitions, all leading us to a giant tear in the ocean, leading him to Jeremiah and to me, leading all of us to each other.

Coop's focus is at my neck. He points at it. "That necklace. Where did you get it?"

"I've always had it," I answer.

Lindy nods. "She had it when I found her."

"Moon snail shells," I say.

"I gave one just like it to Alexis. On our last night together. When we found her . . ." He hesitates. "It was
gone."

Lindy's grip is still a force around my palm. She and
Coop share a sad smile as the ocean swells and falls.

As Jeremiah and his dad head back to Gramzy's, Lindy and I sit in the bunker, the two of us with our backs against the weathered wood.

"She was my sister," Lindy tells me. "And she was gone. And then, nothing was the same again. We didn't come back here."

"Never?" I ask.

She shakes her head. "Nope. My parents became like, I don't know, the shells you collect. Hard and empty, and impossible to get inside."

"Did you see Len and Kimmy again?"

Her voice is sad. "No. I think about them sometimes. I know it was painful for them, too. That night. And after."

"What made you come back?"

"I never thought I would. And then . . ." She looks out, extends her arm toward the shore. "I just drove straight here one day. All the way from Delaware. And I never left."

"Why?"

"I wanted answers. I stayed at the Beachcomber Motel and bought the first house to go on sale on the ocean side. It was just *two* houses away from where it all ended, and I came out to the water every night and I woke every morning waiting for something to, just, *happen*."

"Like what?"

"I don't know. A different outcome to that awful night. And then it did."

"What did?" I ask.

"You."

"And that's how you knew . . . ," I realize.

". . . that you were mine." She finishes the words I've heard over and over and, for the first time, I understand.

"You should have told me about her," I say.

"Maybe. But I wanted to break free of that. I never told anybody who I was to this place. Who I was to that *day*. I had spent so much time just trying to figure out a way to move forward. And then you came. And I could."

"What about Jeremiah's dad?" I ask. *"Coop."* I still can't believe it. "Did you keep in touch?"

She shakes her head. "By the time I got here, he was long gone."

"It wasn't right, what he did. Leaving Jeremiah and all. But maybe I get it."

She nods. "First Alexis . . . then Jeremiah's mom . . ." Her voice trails off. She twirls her fingers around my wet and salty hair, then sighs deeply.

I lean into her arm, the crook of her elbow cradling my neck.

"It makes sense that your dreams would lead us all back here."

I grip the moon snail necklace and hold it out to her. "How is it possible?" I ask. "That I would have the same necklace?"

"The ocean takes a lot of things," she tells me. "Sometimes, it gives them back. I've always thought that you came from *her*."

"Alexis?"

She nods. "Alexis. The ocean. You were born from that summer."

Maybe I was. It doesn't seem so strange. My entire body sinks into the sand, the exhaustion of the night finally settling in.

"Does Elder know about all this?" I ask.

Lindy shakes her head.

I can't believe I'm about to say what I do. "You should tell him."

"It's become this terrible secret," Lindy says. "The bad luck Jeremiah's dad feels . . . I understand that."

"The night you and Alexis went swimming. You and

Kimmy making wishes. The way you tried to save her. It's not all terrible. You should tell him," I repeat. "I mean, you let him into our house. Now let him in, like, for real."

She nods, then laughs. "I could say the same to you. You *could* get to know him, Summer. You might like him."

I groan. "I guess."

"But you're right. It's a big part of my life to just erase."

"I wish you had told me," I say. "But there's something about learning it like this . . ." I nestle deeper into her shoulder. "It's what I always wanted. Ever since you found me."

"What is?" she asks.

"A part of *you* to be a part of *me*."

She smiles. "Always."

"I only wish the ocean could have shown me more."

She sets my twirled hair against my neck and lets her fingers rest there. "There's something you should know, Summer. About that morning."

"What morning?"

"I always said that I *found* you, but . . ." She hesitates. "That's not entirely true."

I feel my heart begin to race.

"I didn't walk the shore and stumble across you there. It wasn't like that. I was at the deck, and I saw you in the water. You came in with the tide. I had to help you." Her voice catches. "I had to help you breathe again."

I try to understand. "I wasn't breathing?" I ask.

She shakes her head. "You had swallowed too much water."

"Wait, so I was *drowning* or something?"

"Drowned," she says.

Drowned?

"I helped you start breathing again, and the paramedics came and you know everything from there. The police. The investigation."

But I can't think of all that. *I wasn't breathing?* "Was there anyone else there?" I ask, my heart drumming.

"Not that I saw. And the detectives knew that. Always. The investigation was thorough. But there was a lot, in all that commotion, I might not have seen."

"What do you mean?" I ask.

"I mean, we never knew *everything* that happened that morning. We couldn't."

"You couldn't," I whisper.

"Maybe I should have told you sooner. But now you know it all." She takes a deep breath. "I'm sorry I didn't."

I feel her fingers resting near my necklace, and I reach for them. *I wasn't breathing and Lindy helped me breathe again.*

I turn to her. "You saved my life."

She squeezes my hand. "More like you saved mine."

LOW TIDE, 4:03 P.M.

"So what do you think of a summer in the mountains?" Jeremiah asks. He sits cross-legged on our kitchen chair with some homework assignment, all sweat-stained from track practice.

Tanvi lies flat on the couch, her arms stretching up above her, holding on to a romance called *Jockeys and Juleps.*

I just rest my elbows at the table with my own homework. Even if it's months away until the end of the school year, I wonder how I'll survive an entire summer without Jeremiah. "Why can't your dad just visit you here again?"

"'Cause I've never been to the mountains."

The reason sounds as good as any. It feels like none of us in Barnes Bluff have ever been anywhere. It's funny that it would be the biggest hermit we knew of, *Turtle Lady,* who'd end up on someone else's shores down in Florida.

I try to imagine where I'd go, but I can't even picture

it. Maybe that's the problem with year-rounders. All this living in a place where everyone else visits. You get stuck in the same endless cycle of seasons, never walking a floor that doesn't have the slightest dusting of sand.

Tanvi reads *loudly,* slapping another page down, as if to scream louder toward *done.* When I told her about Lindy saving me and how all my dreams were real, she called me *the girl who came back from the dead,* and she sank even deeper into stories, if that was possible. I guess she's making sure she knows what love story she wants.

I fumble through my own book. The one we found in Turtle Lady's dumpster, *A Guide to Long Island's Shores.* My new science experiment is becoming more like a history assignment. I'm putting all the shells to use. The oysters and mussels, the moon snails and lady crabs. They're the history of each creature. A reminder of their pasts.

The doorknob rattles, which sets Elsa off. She races along the floorboards, paws scraping the wood, yapping and clucking, rushing the door, then bouncing like a pogo stick.

Elder pushes the door open, a goofy grin plastered across his face, like always. "Hello, Summer and friends." He says it like we're a television sitcom. He grabs Elsa's collar, and she pops up and down like a crazed puppet.

Tanvi is suddenly interested. Her book drops to the floor, and she sits up quick, surveying Elder and Lindy from her spot on the couch.

The Shaky's only open weekdays for lunch in the off-season, serving the fishermen who have already been up a full workday, so Elder drops off and picks up Lindy on the way to and from the hatchery. Lindy's shedding her things, her bag and a funky scarf. She slips her flats off.

I want to close up shop, too, rush my own things up to my room and yank Tanvi and Jeremiah away. But I know that Elder is a part of things now, so I will myself to stay put.

Elder tries to keep Elsa down while holding out a white cardboard box. "I don't want to interrupt your study group, but I thought you might want to take a look at this."

I guess I have to get up and take it, so I make a show of leaving the table, swinging around the chair, huffing, and traveling around Lindy's lump of things. "What is it?"

"I sent away for it. Careful. It's fragile."

As soon as I get close enough, I get the whiff of Elder's awful fish smell from a day at the hatchery and glance at Jeremiah, who is bringing his own hand to his nose.

I try not to grimace as I take the box. It's postmarked from a lab in Australia. Inside, there's tissue paper and Bubble Wrap, and I carefully peel back the layers. It's a shell. But different from any I've seen here. It's in the shape of a coil, but none of its sides touch.

"*Spirula*—" Elder and I both say at the same time.

I look up at him. I didn't think it was possible, but his smile is even goofier. There's an excited tremor in his voice. "It's the one I told you about. I thought since I

211

ruined the mold experiment, you could use this for your assignment."

"It's sixth grade, Elder. This isn't kindergarten show-and-tell," I say, but Lindy squeezes my shoulder, looking over me into the box.

"It's pretty," she says.

I have to agree as I run my fingers over the soft shell. It's nice. He's doing something nice. So I force a half smile. "Thank you. I really like it." I hesitate. "I love it," I confess. Because I do.

We stand there for a minute, in silence. I guess he doesn't get the hint that our moment, or whatever this is, is over, so I make sure to let him know. "We've got to finish our homework," I tell him.

"Oh, right, right. Of course. I'll see you all later, Summer and friends." He does this weird bow thing as he crosses the room, holding tight to Elsa's collar. She's seething as he drags her across the floor to the stairs.

"He's taller than I thought he'd be," Tanvi immediately starts in.

Lindy laughs.

"I can definitely see what you see in him," she continues.

"Tanvi," I scold.

"What? Lindy's all quirky and cool. She needs someone practical. Levelheaded. Science-y. He's nerdy-cute."

Lindy slaps my shoulder, amused. "See?"

I look at Jeremiah, and we roll our eyes at the same time, but I try to understand Lindy and Elder from Tanvi's perspective, as if they are on the tattered cover of one of her paperbacks with the roaring ocean behind them. Maybe it does make sense.

I hold on to the shell. "I'll be right back," I say, then I charge up the stairs myself, the remnants of fish smell wafting down the stairs. I hear the shower start up in the bathroom. Elsa scratches and yelps behind the door of Lindy and Elder's room.

I move toward the bookshelf of my own bedroom, to the arcade tickets and the jar of actual ocean.

I lift it and swish around the murky brown water inside.

Like Lindy said, we couldn't know *everything*. At least, not now. The ocean is an endless study of secrets. Maybe, someday, it will reveal all of the ones that are mine.

For now, I'm glad I came back to life. To *this* life.

I look around at the piles of my funky shell collection and feel for the moon snail shell at my neck. I take out the *Spirula* from its box, from its place in a lab, perfectly white, pristine, and smooth. It's not barnacled or jagged or a mix of faded colors like the others. It sits in a perfect coil, empty of who it used to be.

The ram's horn squid is so rarely seen alive, you'd never even know it existed if it didn't leave its shell behind.

I set it on the shelf, like a secret.

HIGH TIDE, 11:44 A.M.

"I just need to find one more thing," I tell Lindy the next morning, the two of us slopping through the marsh. "And then the science project will be complete. *Plus*"—I point ahead—"you get to see *this*."

We both stop at the overturned canoe. Lindy runs her fingers across the wood. The paint is weathered and faded but there.

"The turtle." She smooths her hand over it. "I wanted Coop to paint a turtle."

"Why?" I ask.

"I don't know. I like turtles."

Our rubber boots squish in the mud.

"I remember wanting so badly for things to go back to the way they were that summer. With Alexis. With Kimmy and Len. I spent a lot of time wishing for it." She

214

cups her fingers under my chin and turns me to face her. "Promise me you won't do that."

I wince a little, knowing I've spent time wishing Elder away, wishing we could go back to the two of us, and Lindy knows that.

She drops my chin from her hand. "You can miss stuff. That's allowed."

I laugh. "*Allowed?* Like you can control *missing.*"

"It just shouldn't stop you from moving forward. That's all. I might have closed out the past, but imagine if I stopped moving forward after Alexis was gone. Imagine all I would have missed." She twirls her fingers in my hair.

I look into the shallow pools of water, the way they ripple at the slightest hint of movement. *Watch your step,* Turtle Lady had warned.

"They should be somewhere over here," I say. I scoot down low. "This is where Turtle Lady told me about them."

Lindy crouches down, looking with me.

"She was the one making sure they survived before she left. I have to make sure they made it."

I carefully scour the small tidal pools until I find the white and pinkish eggs, jagged-toothed and broken in the sand, and my heart beats, *no, no, no,* praying they haven't been ruined and crushed.

I dig softly around them. All that's left are three broken

shells. I sigh, relieved. "They hatched," I tell Lindy. "They're gone."

"I hope they're okay."

I look out, across the marsh toward the shore, as if I could see the terrapins scurrying away, but of course I can't. "They are. They have to be. It's the way of things."

Lindy kneels beside me and we both reach out at the same time to collect the soft eggshell remains. A gift of the ocean that's ours.

ACKNOWLEDGMENTS

Thank you to my editor, Julia Maguire, for understanding what I was trying to do with this story and guiding it forward with your remarkable insight. I feel so lucky to work with you. Rebecca Stead, thank you for being there every step of the way with warmth, humor, and kindness. You always have just the right words when my writer's soul is weary.

Allison Wortche, this book would not be a book without your enthusiasm for my work. To everyone at Knopf and Random House, I am thankful for all you've done to bring my stories into the world, packaged with such love and care.

To early readers of Summer's story: Lori, Emma,

Susannah, Stuart, and Carys, I am grateful for your notes and thoughts. Jennifer Justice, I appreciate your help understanding more about adoption and foster care. Alison Cherry, thank you for the gift of your starfish story.

To the Electric 18s, I would not have survived my first year as an author without your energy and support. Laurie Morrison, I am so grateful for your friendship. Thank you for reading Summer's story and helping me find the right ending. Jennifer Chen, your hard work and dedication inspire me more than you know. Thank you for holding me accountable. Writing *Done* is never as satisfying without you on the other side.

To my Goats: you are community, light, and love. Thank you for always being there. Sabrina Enayatulla, Gwen Glazer, and Rebecca Fishman, thanks for helping me feel less alone at my desk by letting me rope you into the publishing process. Bonnie Becker, this book would not exist without the hours of love and care you gave to Emily.

Thank you to Tracy, Christine, Brian, Tara, Kim, and Scott for carefree summers on Layton Avenue. Jennifer Bezmen, I wonder if you remember the pickles. You are all at the heart of this story.

Mom and Dad, thank you for Mondays and for a lifetime of love. Lynn Reed and Brad Reed, thanks for all of your support.

Tyler, Owen, and Emily, thank you for inspiring me every day with your bright and open hearts.